JUST FOR TONIGHT

BREAKING THE RULES
BOOK 2

CADENCE KEYS

Copyright © 2024 by Cadence Keys

All rights reserved.

No part of this book may be reproduced in any form or by any electronic or mechanical means, including information storage and retrieval systems, without written permission from the author, except for the use of brief quotations in a book review.

This book is a work of fiction. Names, characters, places, and incidents are a product of the author's imagination. Locales and public names are sometimes used for atmospheric purposes. Any resemblances to actual people, living or dead, businesses, companies, events, institutions, or locales are entirely coincidental. Any trademarks, service marks, product names, or named features are assumed to be the property of their respective owners and are used only for reference.

Editors: Happily Editing Anns

Cover Design: Cadence Keys

Special Edition Cover: Lily Bear Design Co.

*To all my romance girlies who want a man who will rail
them hard and then make them dinner.*

Rule #1

DON'T HAVE SEX WITH A STRANGER IN A BAR BATHROOM

JENNA

I threw the shot back and then slammed the glass down on the counter, wincing at the bartender's stern glare. Yeah, breaking a shot glass was not on the agenda tonight.

I was here to get laid.

To have a one-night stand to be more precise.

And I'd never needed liquid courage more in my life.

If my best friend, Sadie, was here, she'd tell me I didn't need to go through with this, but she didn't understand. She was blissfully in love. With my dad, of all people.

Gross.

No, she didn't understand at all.

She didn't understand what it was like to date a guy for four years—the same guy you gave your virginity to—thinking he was going to be the man you marry only for him to dump you and then start dating someone else a week later. She didn't know what it was like to go years without sex like I now had. She didn't question her bedroom skills like I did or ache for *something*, unable to articulate what that something actually was.

All I knew was that sex with Peter had been...okay, but I was pretty sure sex was supposed to be better than okay. It was supposed to be toe-curling, mind-blowing, life-altering. I wanted passion, adventure, a fucking orgasm from penetration for fuck's sake.

I shook my empty shot glass at the bartender, and he came over and poured another with a slight arch of his dark brow. He was attractive, but I'm pretty sure he could tell I was a train wreck waiting to happen.

I was here to make bad choices, and I was worried it showed all over my face.

Not that I thought one-night stands were bad choices for everyone. I just didn't think they were for me, but what the fuck did I know? I'd been with the same guy, the only guy, for four years, and then abstinent for another two while working on getting my veterinary degree—something else that hit my confidence hard.

Maybe I was about to discover that I was a one-night stand pro.

It was possible.

I tipped the glass back, swallowing down the liquid and relishing in the warm tingle as it went down my throat. With the effects of the alcohol starting to firm up my resolve, I spun on the barstool and perused my options.

Before I had a chance to look for more than a few seconds, my phone buzzed in my purse, which I could feel against my leg. I dug in my bag and glanced at the screen only to roll my eyes and toss it back in. It was my mother and I couldn't deal with her right now. I was on a mission and didn't need to hear about her new husband—who I'd never met because she'd been with him less than a month.

I doubted he'd last long enough that it would even be worth my time to meet him in the first place, but I'd reluctantly promised to have brunch with them tomorrow morning. That was all she was getting from me. My mother stole enough of my peace on a daily basis; I wasn't about to let her ruin tonight when I'd finally gotten enough courage to pursue an anonymous hookup.

But my mom was tomorrow's problem. Tonight I needed to stay focused on my mission. There was a group of polo-wearing dude bros throwing flirty glances at a group of blondes.

Hard pass.

They all looked too much like my classic boy-next-door ex. Sadie had said I needed someone different and she was right.

Different was exactly what I needed.

So, I focused on guys with dark hair, which was about the time prickles climbed the back of my neck—the good kind, the kind that held promise and possibility. I glanced to my right, and there at the end of the bar was a man who immediately made my stomach knot and my lady bits tingle.

His hair was cut close to his scalp—a military cut if I ever saw one. His dark eyes watched me with hunger as he held a glass of amber liquid close to his lips before the right side of his mouth tilted up ever so slightly in the cockiest smirk I had ever seen. He tossed what was left of his drink back in one gulp, then gently placed it down on the counter and stood from his stool. His walk was filled with confidence and swagger, and each step closer made my panties wetter.

This was a man who exuded sex, but it was the confidence which bordered on cocky that made excitement thrum in my belly.

This man.

He was exactly the kind of man who would excel at an anonymous hookup. I bet he was a pro at unattached sex.

I stayed in my seat, even though I had to actively fight my body's desire to fidget under his penetrating gaze. His dark brown eyes slid down my body before sliding back up, and I held my breath. For a moment, my determination wavered.

What if he found me lacking?

What if I was cold and boring like Peter had implied?

What if I was bad at sex?

By the time he reached me, my posture had withered slightly, and the knots in my stomach were no longer from desire, but from trepidation.

His eyes narrowed as he reached me and then that cocky smirk grew.

"Don't get shy on me now, darlin'."

Oh my God, heaven help me, he had an accent. His thick southern twang came out smooth as butter and melted all my unease. Fuck me, but I was a sucker for a man with an accent.

If he called me sugar, I might fall off this stool.

He moved in closer, his lips grazing my ear. "Whatever's goin' on in that head of yours, I can fuck it out of you."

God, he was bold. And maybe for another woman it would be a turnoff, but for me, it was exactly what I needed.

With a surge of adrenaline, I pulled back enough to make eye contact. "Is that a promise?"

His eyes flared with heat, and any hesitancy I had evaporated.

"Oh, darlin', you bet your fine ass it is."

"And how are you gonna do that?" I didn't know who I

was right now, but I was thankful for this playful boldness that was so completely out of character for me.

That smirk made another appearance and he glanced around the room, his gaze locking on something to our left. I followed his line of sight to the sign for the restrooms.

"You game?"

Stealing some of his confidence, I slid off my stool, grazing his body in the process, and then walked straight to the bathrooms. I didn't glance behind me, and there was a chance he was just standing by the bar watching me look like a complete fool, but I was going to trust my gut on this one.

I pushed open the door of the women's bathroom which was blessedly empty. The door had barely shut when it opened again and he came inside, closing it and flipping the lock. His dark eyes stared me down, and he shook his head slowly before rubbing his hand along his sharp, chiseled jaw.

"You're unexpected, ya know that?"

"Good unexpected?" I asked, thankful my voice didn't quiver and reveal how out of my depth I was.

His gaze locked on mine as he closed the distance between us. He wrapped his hand around the back of my neck. "Oh yeah."

And then his lips were on mine. He kissed me like he'd already commanded every private part of my body, like he knew me intimately. It was a kiss that demanded submission. His lips were firm and his tongue rough as he pushed it into my mouth. I accepted it willingly, a moan escaping as my knees shook from the pure possession of his kiss.

My fingers gripped his forearms, holding him tightly, still afraid this was a dream and he was going to pull back any moment.

This was the single best kiss of my life, and there was no way I was letting him pull away now.

But pulling away appeared to be the last thing on his mind. Instead, he growled, gripping my thighs and lifting me up. My legs automatically wrapped around his waist as we crashed against the wall. One of his hands moved under my ass to continue holding me as he ground his thick, hard length against where I wanted him most. The other came up and held my throat, gripping ever so slightly—not enough to hurt, but enough for me to know he was in charge.

I should've been surprised, or maybe alarmed—no man had ever done that to me before—but instead, my clit throbbed and my panties were soaked.

"Lift up that skirt for me, darlin', and show me that pussy I'm dying to get inside."

I moaned, my hips gyrating against his with a nearly uncontrollable urge. It felt so good to rub against the seam of his jeans. But I was also eager to feel him, so I unwrapped my hands from his neck and shimmied my skirt up as he held me firmly between his body and the wall.

We both looked down at the wet spot on the front of his jeans where I'd been grinding against him.

"Fuck, you are perfect," he said, his voice so ragged my confidence soared.

I did that to him.

"Wanna taste?"

He growled again before slamming his lips on mine in a punishing kiss. "You're goddamn right I want a taste."

With a gentleness that was unexpected from his gruff demeanor, he set me on my feet before squatting down and pulling my panties to the side. In the next breath, his lips were sucking on my pussy lips, and my hands were holding on to his head for dear life as I fought against the loud moan threatening to escape.

Oh my God.

My thighs shook as he worked his magic with his tongue. Then he slid one long finger inside my tight channel, and stars burst across my vision as my legs tightened and my body convulsed against his mouth.

Through the haze of my mind-bending orgasm, I heard him moan against my pussy before pulling back. My breath caught at the way his lips glistened with my juices. I didn't think the sight had ever been sexy before, but on this guy it was.

He pushed a second finger inside me, then a third, stretching me wide, and then placed a kiss on my clit—a kiss that was more tender than I expected from a man like him.

"Your taste is dangerous, darlin', and fucking addictive. I could bury my head in this sweet pussy all night."

Yes, please.

His gaze lit with mirth, and that cocky smirk made another appearance. Oh shit, did I say that out loud?

He stood up and adjusted the thick length in his pants before pinning me in place with his hot gaze.

"I'm not done with you by a long shot, but I can't do all the things I want to do to this hot little body in a bar bathroom. Your place or mine, Sugar?"

Oh for fuck's sake. He called me sugar.

This was by far the most reckless thing I'd ever done, but there was no way I was stopping it now. So even though I knew it wasn't wise to go somewhere with a complete stranger, I also knew I didn't want him to know where I lived.

I wanted him to fuck my brains out tonight and then never see him again. And I was determined to get what I wanted.

Rule #2

DON'T BE VULNERABLE WITH A ONE-NIGHT STAND

JENNA

His place ended up being a hotel nearby. He didn't explain and I didn't ask. This was an anonymous hookup. We didn't need to know anything about each other except for what made the other moan.

Instead of talking, the second we walked through the door, he had one hand on my throat and the other pulling up my dress and sliding into my panties where he found me still soaking wet for him. I moaned as he rubbed gentle circles on my clit that were like torture because they were too light to get me off but heavy enough to tease.

"Fuck, I love the sounds you make. I want you to scream for me tonight."

"What about the neighbors?" This wasn't the nicest hotel in the world—probably a solid three stars—and in my experience, even nice hotels tended to have thin walls, which meant these were likely paper thin.

"Fuck the neighbors. You want to be my little slut tonight and we both know it."

He groaned as his words caused another round of arousal to flood where his fingers were buried in my pussy, proving his words right. I didn't mind him calling me his little slut—even if the degradation of it should've bothered me, but somehow it turned me on more than anything ever had in my life.

Then his lips were on mine and his tongue was plundering my mouth again, and any words I could've come up with were completely lost.

He had me naked in seconds, but then took his time kissing every inch of my body, whispering dirty words that made my pussy throb and ache for him to stuff me full like he promised. Each kiss felt like he was discovering a new erogenous zone that left me needy and desperate.

"Please," I begged. "I need you."

It was the truth. He'd already made me feel more sexually satisfied than my ex had in our four years together. I was desperate to feel what he could do to me with that big cock in his pants.

He let out a low growl that was sexy as hell and then he was ripping off his clothes. We stood a foot apart, and my eyes grew wide at the sight of his naked body. He was by far the fittest guy I'd ever seen naked. His six-pack was solid like a rock, and his arms were a gift from the big man himself, as if molded from clay by the most superior artist in the history of the world. Every muscle, every inch of his body was sculpted to perfection. His thick thighs were a sign that he never skipped leg day, but it was the monster between his legs that had me feeling faint.

Holy shit, he was hung.

"That's not gonna fit."

There was that smirk again, and when I finally met his

gaze, there was a dare in his eyes that made my heart beat faster.

"It'll fit, especially as wet as you are already," he said, his voice low and gruff.

He closed the small distance and shoved a hand into my hair at the base of my neck, his gaze locked on mine. I couldn't decipher the look in his eyes. It was more than heat and lust, though.

"This is just for tonight," I murmured, reminding him—and myself—that this couldn't go any further, even if our chemistry was off the charts. Even if he made me feel a chaotic desperation I'd never experienced before.

Even if he'd already proven he could command my body in a way no man ever had.

"Get on the bed."

I scampered to the bed and lay back as he walked slowly to me like a predator eyeing his prey.

His jaw clenched as he stared at me, his gaze sliding up and down my body. He rubbed his jaw and looked around the room before looking back at me. He walked to the edge of the bed and grabbed each of my wrists, bringing them together and holding them firmly against the pillow above my head.

"No matter what, leave your hands right here. Understand?"

I nodded.

"Nuh-uh, darlin'. I'm gonna need you to say it."

"I understand."

Was that my voice that was all breathy?

"Good girl."

Oh fuck, another surge of wetness pooled at my entrance. His free hand slid over my breasts, tweaking a nipple until it bordered on pain, and then he bent over and sucked it into his mouth. His teeth nipped at it, and my back arched off the bed as a loud moan was set free from my throat.

Holy shit.

"Fuck, you're so responsive."

"Sorry," I mumbled, my cheeks heating with embarrassment.

He pulled away until his fierce gaze latched on to mine, and I couldn't look away if I tried.

"Don't ever fucking apologize for your sounds, Sugar. They're the sexiest thing I've ever heard. And if a man can't handle your noises, then you better dump his stupid ass. Got it?"

I swallowed thickly, fighting against the unexpected emotion rising to the surface. Peter constantly criticized me when I made too much noise. He always made me feel silly for them, saying they sounded fake, as if I was trying too hard. I'd started to think something was wrong with me because most of the time I couldn't help it.

But here was this complete stranger telling me it was a turn-on, calling me perfect, making my body hum with so much pleasure, it almost felt like too much. Who the hell was this guy? And how the hell was I supposed to keep my walls up when he was washing away years of self-doubt with his words and hungry gaze? He was making me feel more confident in my body and myself than I had in years.

I nodded because I couldn't speak over the lump in my throat, but that appeared to be enough for him.

He ducked back down and nipped at my other nipple, but this time, he didn't let go right away. He didn't let go until his free hand had slid down to the apex of my thighs and he could feel how wet I was. He released his hold on my nipple with his teeth and then he sucked hard as his thumb circled my clit and two fingers slid inside me, rubbing against a spot that only he'd ever been able to find.

My body shook as another orgasm cascaded over me.

"Scream for me, dirty girl."

I couldn't hold it back if I tried. The scream ripped from my throat as my orgasm seemed to go on forever. I felt a rush of fluid as my legs shook, and my body felt like it was transported to another universe. When it finally subsided, I sagged into the mattress. As I came back to earth, mortification took over whatever pleasure I'd felt.

I tried to pull my hands from his strong grip so I could cover my face and hide the tears that were already beginning to stream down my face.

"Hey, hey," he said, lying down next to me and caressing my skin. I'd never felt more exposed or vulnerable or embarrassed in my entire life. "What's goin' on?"

I kept my eyes closed because I couldn't bear to see the pity or reproach I was sure would be in his eyes.

"I'm sorry. That's never happened before," I choked out.

"You've never squirted before?" There was a hint of something in his tone that had me reluctantly opening my eyes.

His gaze was lit with what looked suspiciously like superiority and happiness.

"Squirted?" Is that what they call peeing yourself during sex?

His smile morphed into that stupid sexy smirk from the bar.

"Yeah, darlin', and I'm not sure why you're upset because that was hot."

"What?"

He leaned down and kissed me, this time with a tender

passion that wasn't there before, like he was comforting me. For the first time tonight, I wished I knew his name.

"It's normal. And hot, in my opinion. I kinda want to try to see if I can get you to squirt on my cock." His voice got lower and more ragged. "I bet your pussy would grip me so tight I'd come harder than I ever have."

"You liked it?" I had to be sure.

"Darlin', I fucking loved it. Let's try to do it again."

And he did. After he kissed and sucked on every inch of my body again until I was pliant and yet wound up at the same time, he slid a condom on and fucked me so hard, I saw stars and squirted all over his huge, monster cock.

And just like he predicted, he came hard, collapsing beside me like my pussy had just sucked his soul from his body.

Then ten minutes later, we did it again.

For hours, he fucked me like I'd only imagined in my dreams. Teaching me that I not only liked rough, dirty sex— I *loved* it. We couldn't seem to stop until the dawn arrived and we both collapsed from pure exhaustion. He passed out quickly, and even though I was spent, I knew I needed to leave. This was only supposed to be one night, and with the rising sun, our night was officially over.

I was also worried if I was still here when he woke up, I'd ask his name. I'd want another night. And then another.

He was that addictive.

I opened the door to his room as quietly as possible, but as I took a step out into the hall, I couldn't stop myself from turning back and getting one last look at the man I knew without a shadow of a doubt I'd never forget.

His face was lax with sleep and he looked peaceful. I fought against the urge to leave him a note, to tell him my name, but that's not what last night was.

It was a one-night stand.

As I quietly closed the door and made my way home, I reminded myself that this was why I didn't do one-night stands. I wasn't a girl who could do unattached sex.

After one incredible night, I was already attached to my nameless man.

I was trying not to mourn the loss of something that was never really mine to begin with, but I already knew that even if I was never going to see him again, I'd never forget him.

Rule #3

A ONE-NIGHT STAND MEANS YOU NEVER HAVE TO SEE THEM AGAIN

JENNA

Brunch with my mom was the last thing I wanted to do on such little sleep, but after taking a nap, I showered off the sweat residue and smell of sex and got dressed in a comfortable summer dress with a fitted cardigan over it. I knew my mom would likely have something negative to say about my outfit—she always did—but I couldn't bring myself to care today.

I was still reeling from the night before. My body was sore in ways I'd never experienced, my muscles burning with each movement and my sex aching from the stretch of his huge dick. Two years without anything but my vibrator was no match for the giant cock that owned my body last night.

The drive to the restaurant my mom had chosen went by in a blur. When I pulled up, a valet came running to take my car—because of course my mom would choose a restaurant with valet service. Heaven forbid she park her own car.

How she and my dad ever got together in the first place would forever remain a mystery to me.

I handed the valet my keys, choosing to ignore the look he gave my outfit which didn't scream wealth in the slightest. I was a poor grad student; I wasn't going to pretend I was anything else. At least it was a dress and not my favorite jeans I'd been eyeing while I was getting dressed.

I walked into the restaurant and immediately saw my mom sitting at a table near the window. I assumed the man sitting next to her was her new husband. I couldn't believe she went off and eloped after knowing the guy a month.

Actually, I could. It wasn't the first time my mom had done something this crazy. She was a serial gold digger. She dated and married men like she was trying out different ice cream flavors at Baskin-Robbins.

I wondered how long this one would last.

"Hey Mom," I said as I approached the table.

Her eyes lit up and she smiled as wide as she could, even if the rest of her face didn't move much, thanks to her regular Botox injections. My mom was nothing if not the stereotypical vapid Beverly Hills wife.

"My baby! I'm so glad you were able to make it."

She would have guilt-tripped me for days if I hadn't.

"Jenna, this is Richard Jackson."

He stood and extended his hand. "All my friends call me Dick."

I bit the inside of my cheek to stop myself from saying something embarrassing like why on earth a man would choose to be called a body part instead of Rich or his full name, Richard. I reached out and took his hand. He had a firm grip at least, better than the last guy my mom dated who had a weak-ass handshake and even weaker morals.

He'd cheated on her within a few days of them getting together.

"Nice to meet you."

He gestured for me to sit in one of the two seats across from them, so I did.

God, this was awkward. It always was, but I was so not in the mood today, and it was hard to fake enthusiasm or interest like I usually did.

"I'm so glad you decided to come back down to LA for the summer," my mom said.

My pasted smile faltered slightly, but she didn't notice. "Me too," I said weakly.

If only she knew the reason I moved home was because I was struggling in my classes, and my advisor had recommended I take the summer off to regroup before fall semester. So, while my peers were all working internships at local veterinary offices, I was down here in LA, lazing around in the apartment I'd managed to sublet from a friend I met in undergrad who was out of the country for the summer.

I was taking a sip of my water when Dick—nope, I couldn't even *think* that name without wanting to giggle inappropriately—smiled wide at something or someone behind me.

"Hey! You made it," he said as he stood.

I spun around in my chair and then froze in my seat, my eyes bugging out like they do in those old-school cartoons.

What in the actual fuck?

"Jenna, meet my son, Connor."

His son?!

Oh my fucking God. I wished the floor would swallow me whole or that I'd never agreed to come to this disaster of a brunch.

Because his son—*Connor*— was none other than the same man who rearranged my insides during the best sex of my entire life last night.

Monster dick had a name, and worse than that, he was my new stepbrother.

Fuck me.

Connor's steps didn't falter as he moved to the table, but his eyes never left mine.

"Connor, this is Jenna, Vanessa's daughter."

The son of a bitch—actually, his mom was probably lovely unless she was as vapid as mine, but that was beside the point—had the audacity to pull out that cocky smirk that had my panties wet last night. My traitorous body lit up like the Fourth of July, and that delicious ache that I felt with every step pulsed at the reminder of all the naughty things we had done.

The way he held my throat firmly as he thrust deep inside me.

The way he called me his dirty little slut and had me coming on his cock until I saw stars.

The way he praised me each and every time I squirted.

My cheeks flamed with a blush that made sweat bead at my temple. My heart raced and I was struggling to breathe.

Oh my God.

Oh my God.

Oh my fucking God.

I had sex with my new stepbrother.

Rule #4

DON'T FLIRT WITH NEW RELATIVES

CONNOR

I'd woken up in a shit mood for multiple reasons.

One, I had promised to meet my dad's new wife today, despite knowing the odds of this marriage lasting any longer than the others were slim to none.

Two, the beautiful woman who'd come out of nowhere and blown me wide open with the best sex of my fucking life had been gone when I woke up. She didn't even leave a note.

I knew we'd said it was just for one night, but fuck. She was...goddamn perfect. I'd never met anyone who set me on fire the way she did with just a look. Add in her body and that fucking sinful mouth and I was a goner.

But then I showed up at this fancy-ass restaurant and who did I find at the table with my dad and new stepmom?

My mystery woman, who looked even sexier this morning than I remembered. I knew under that modest outfit was a very dirty woman who had squeezed my dick so hard last night I thought her pussy was going to break it off my damn body.

And now I was hard.

"Connor?" My dad frowned at me, probably because I'd frozen in my spot and couldn't stop staring at my woman from last night. My mood turned around instantly, and I couldn't hold back my grin as I held out my hand, as if I hadn't touched and licked every inch of her perfect body.

"Connor."

She glanced back at her mom and my dad and then hesitantly reached out and took my hand. I didn't miss the way her breath stuttered at the connection. I knew she felt it too—the instant zing from our touch. She was trying to remain composed and not give away that we'd spent hours naked together last night. But I'd made a study of her body's response to me in just those few hours, and the way her cheeks flushed and she nibbled her bottom lip nervously gave away that she was nowhere near as composed as she wanted to be.

"Jenna," she said, her voice soft, almost timid. But I knew better. I knew she could be loud.

Fuck, I loved her sounds.

I reluctantly pulled my hand away, because if I held on any longer, she'd likely glance down and notice the huge, hard bulge in my pants. I took a seat next to her and pulled the seat as close to the table as I could before I leaned back in my chair.

The laid-back posture was fake. I didn't like the position of this chair. Or the table for that matter. It was in the middle of the rows next to the window, and I preferred a seat that allowed me to have my back covered and gave me a clear view of the room.

Courtesy of my time as an Army Ranger, I was a paranoid motherfucker. Never leave your back unprotected.

"How was your flight?" Dad asked.

"Fine."

"Connor, your dad tells me you just got out of the army. What are your plans now?" My new stepmom fit Dad's usual MO. Straight, dark hair, heavy makeup that was supposed to look natural while hiding every minor imperfection that would *actually* look natural, and designer clothes.

The man had a type, that was for damn sure.

"I'm looking into some things."

"Where are you staying while you're here?" Dad asked.

I took a sip of my water and fought against the irritation tickling my spine. I hated getting the third degree, but this game of twenty questions was starting to feel like exactly that.

"I was at a hotel last night, but I'll be staying in Grant's guest room for a while."

Grant Davis and I had been best friends since we were in diapers. We'd been inseparable until I joined the army and he went to college, but we kept in touch throughout the years. He was working his dream job as an architect at a small firm here in Los Angeles.

"How is Grant?" Dad asked, although I wasn't sure he truly cared. He never cared about any of my friends. Most of the time I wasn't even convinced he cared about me. I'd been the only child of two people who'd stayed together for appearances until they couldn't stand it anymore, and only had me because it was what you did after you got married, not because they'd necessarily wanted me.

"Fine."

Dad's face morphed to irritated, and now that was a

look from him I was much more familiar with. I'd always been the disappointment. Heaven forbid that changed now.

"You know you could give more than one-word answers," he muttered.

I could, but I probably wouldn't. Besides, no one here really gave a shit about me, and I was more interested in the woman next to me.

"So, *Jenna.*" I emphasized her name with my signature smirk and my chest tightened at the light flush that filled her cheeks. "What do you do?"

"I'm a grad student," she said primly. Fuck, I loved that little condescending arch of her brow. I wanted to fuck it right off her face.

"Jenna's going to be a veterinarian," her mom preened.

I'd gotten used to reading people, and the way Jenna's gaze dropped to her lap made me think something about that statement wasn't entirely accurate. Did she not want to be a vet?

"Do you go to school around here?"

"No, I go to UC Sacramento up north. I'm just in LA for the summer."

I frowned. She didn't live down here? That wasn't ideal, especially since I had plans to repeat last night—as many times as possible.

The waiter arrived to get our order before I had a chance to ask her more questions. Everyone else ordered first while I skimmed the menu and picked a meat lover's omelet.

When the waiter left, Jenna scooted her chair back. "If you'll excuse me, I'm gonna go wash up before we eat."

She scurried away from the table like her ass was on fire. But she couldn't run from me anymore.

"Ya know, that's a good idea. I think I'll do the same. Be back."

I didn't wait for a response from my dad or his new trophy wife. My only interest in staying for this brunch was speed walking down the hallway toward the ladies' room.

She pushed the door open, and without hesitating a beat, I followed her in. She spun around and her eyes widened, but not with outrage. No, that flush on her cheeks and the way her chest was heaving made it clear she wasn't mad. I'd wager all the money in my bank account that she was turned on.

I held up one finger as she opened her mouth, and she snapped it shut with indignation as she put her hands on her hips. Instead of telling her she looked like Superman standing like that, I bent down and checked to make sure there was nobody in the three stalls in here.

Empty.

With more confidence than I probably should've had, I flipped the lock on the door and then focused all my attention on her.

Jenna.

Knowing her name did something to me. My jaw clenched as I stalked toward her. She backed away from me slowly, but her gaze never left mine, and then she hit the sink and had nowhere else to go.

I didn't speak until we were only a breath apart. "You snuck out this morning without so much as a goodbye." My voice was gruff with desire.

She swallowed thickly, and I had the crazy urge to watch her throat do that same motion while my cock was deep in her mouth. "It was only supposed to be one night. No names. Remember?"

"But I know your name now."

Her eyes flared and her nipples peaked underneath her bra. I placed my hand on the middle of her chest and then slid it up slowly, giving her time to push me away.

She didn't.

My hand held her throat loosely before I brought my thumb up to skim her chin. Fuck me, she was beautiful. Hazel eyes that were a mix of honey brown and jade green. I could've stared into them all day, but we didn't have the time.

There was so much I wanted to do to her, do *with* her, but I knew she was freaking out. She wasn't ready for a push, not yet. But she was too tempting to resist completely. I leaned forward slowly, my gaze locked on hers. Her breath grew heavy the closer I got until my lips barely brushed hers. My heart raced and my need for her grew, but I just held my lips against hers.

"Goddamn, I fucking love your mouth," I murmured, aching to kiss her but using all my self-control to hold myself back.

A small whimper escaped from deep in her throat as she leaned forward infinitesimally. I wondered if she realized that she was the one pushing us closer together now and not me.

"Do you know the things we could do in this bathroom? The way I could make you shudder and fall apart while our parents are just outside that door."

Her pupils dilated, and I fought against the urge to smile. Whether she liked it or not, her body wasn't bothered by my new label. "I could get on my knees, lift your dress, and suck your plump little clit into my mouth until you could barely hold back your scream. I could shove my cock in your tight little pussy so deep and hard, you'd squirt all over us and flood this damn bathroom. And then

I'd lick you clean like you were the best dessert I've ever tasted."

She shuddered against me and her eyes grew heavy-lidded.

"But you don't want that, right? Because I'm your new stepbrother?"

She'd been tipsy last night, but the way her eyes were slightly glazed made me think she was drunk on my words in a way she'd never been on alcohol—at least not last night. She shook her head as if she was trying to shake away a fog.

"Right," she whispered.

I held still for one last second, soaking in the way her body felt pressed against mine, our lips barely touching and her body heat warming me to my core even through our layers of clothes.

Being close to Jenna was like taking the first full breath of air after running through a smoke-filled burning building. She was bringing me back to life and she didn't have a clue.

I stepped back, watching the way the cool air in the space where I'd been cleared the haze out of her eyes. Her chest heaved, but she didn't say a word.

She didn't have to.

She wasn't ready for this, for what we could be. She was too in her head about labels and propriety. It was obvious in the way she held herself back though she'd been so forward and willing last night when she thought she'd never see me again.

But I knew my dad, and his track record for marriages was like clockwork. If she was worried about the step-brother label, then maybe I'd bide my time until I wasn't her stepbrother anymore.

Or I'd find a way to convince her this was worth repeating.

Either way, there was no way in hell I was done with this woman.

"I understand." It wasn't a lie. I understood her immediate concern, but it didn't change the long game for me.

She nodded and then moved to the door. She didn't look back at me as she said, "I'll go out first, so it doesn't look weird that we're coming back together."

I let her go, even as my fingers itched to reach out and grab her.

The door closed, and I leaned my hands on the sink ledge, staring myself down in the mirror. My cheeks were flushed and my eyes a little dilated, but I doubted my dad or his trophy wife would notice.

I thought I'd been rocked from what happened before I was honorably discharged from the army, but it turned out Jenna had the ability to alter my world even more.

And it appeared I'd rocked hers as well, since she was nowhere to be found when I got back to the table. Nope, turned out she'd made a lame excuse and left.

That was okay. I could be patient when I had to be. And for a woman like Jenna, I had no problem waiting a long-ass time for her to realize that the kind of explosive chemistry we had didn't come around every day.

We weren't done by a long shot.

Rule #5

DON'T AGREE TO HAVE SEX WITH YOUR NEW STEPBROTHER

JENNA

I woke up bright and early—too early—the next morning. My brain was a mess of endless memories of Connor's mouth, fingers, and his gloriously large cock. It was so wrong.

He was my *stepbrother*!

I should absolutely not be having filthy, dirty thoughts about my new stepbrother. Even if it was by far the best sex of my entire life.

My nipples peaked as I remembered the way he gripped my throat and whispered dirty words in my ear. Why did that turn me on so much?

Shouldn't I feel dirty and degraded?

Because if that's how I was *supposed* to feel, it wasn't working. I felt...sated. And that wasn't good either.

Connor was a no-go zone. All I could hope for at this point was that my mom's marriage lasted as long as all the others, which meant by this time next month, she'd be divorced and I'd never have to see Connor again.

Rolling out of bed, I threw on some yoga pants and my oversized UC Sacramento sweatshirt and then wandered into the kitchen to make some coffee.

"No. No, no, no. Not today," I mumbled, staring at the empty box next to my Keurig where my coffee pods usually sat. In all the craziness of the past two days, I'd forgotten that I ran out of coffee yesterday morning. I'd planned to get some after brunch with my mom, but then Connor happened.

Okay, not the end of the world. Fortunately, there was a cute coffee shop just down the street. The walk was only about five minutes, and the smell of fresh brewed coffee hit me as soon as I walked through the door. I could already feel my shoulders relaxing just from being in the presence of caffeine.

"Jenna?"

I blamed my lack of coffee for not recognizing the voice right away. But there was no way to hide my shock when I spun around to find Peter standing behind me with his arm wrapped around the slim waist of a petite blonde.

"Peter! Wow. It's been...a while."

He smiled ruefully. "Yeah, it has. How've you been?"

"Fine. I mean great. I've been great." I was lying through my teeth. My life was a hot mess express and *great* was the last word I'd use to describe it, but I already knew I didn't look nearly as put together as these two, so I was not about to share how my life was one disaster away from falling apart.

His smile grew and my stomach cramped. I hadn't seen him since he dumped me, but he looked just as good as I remembered. He had the stereotypical California blond prep boy good looks, and the woman at his side fit him perfectly.

"I'm so glad to hear that," he said, sounding genuine. "Oh man, where are my manners? Jenna, this is my wife, Tiffany."

A record scratch went off in my brain.

His wife? He was married?!

I pasted my smile to my face while I took a better look at her, but all I saw were all the things I lacked. She was pristine with her glossy blonde hair, trim waist, and color-coordinated outfit, while I looked like I'd skipped laundry day and a shower one too many days in a row.

"Next!"

Saved by the barista, I spun back around, quickly placed my order, and then moved toward the end of the bar while my brain tried to organize this information.

My ex was married. He got married. I wondered how many times I'd have to say it before it felt real.

I didn't love Peter anymore, but that didn't change the fact that I'd spent four years of my life—my entire undergrad experience—with him, thinking that someday I'd be the woman he introduced to people as his wife.

And now he was married to someone else.

While I was subletting an apartment from a friend and trying to figure out if I could hack it in veterinary school or if I needed to find a new dream.

Peter and his wife walked over to join me, but thank every higher power in existence that the barista called out my name as soon as they reached me.

"That's me," I said, grabbing my coffee. "So nice seeing you again. Have a good one," I said as I made my way to the exit. If he responded, I didn't notice because I was already racing down the block back to my apartment.

This day was already off to a bad start, and the idea of

hiding in my apartment so it couldn't get any worse was sounding pretty damn good right about now.

Except when I saw who was leaning against the wall next to the door of my building, I had a sinking suspicion my day was only about to get worse.

"How did you find out where I live?" I asked Connor, whose casual pose held a tension that made me think it wasn't all that casual.

"Your mom was more than happy to give me your address," he said, pushing off the wall and moving until we stood in front of each other, my head tilted back to meet his eyes.

God, why did he have to be so tall?

And sexy.

Heat curled in my gut from the memory of his mouth on my body and the wicked things he did with his tongue.

Something was seriously wrong with me.

"She was?" I asked, trying to bring my focus back to our conversation. I knew there was more to it than that. My mom never did anything without an ulterior motive.

He cocked his head side to side. "Well, probably only because it directly benefits her that I'm here. No offense, but your mom is pretty self-absorbed. I wouldn't be giving out my daughter's address to a guy I just met, no matter if he's her new husband's son or not. No offense," he tacked on, as if I could be offended by somebody acknowledging how selfish my mom was.

"None taken. So, how does this benefit her exactly?"

"She wants us to plan a reception for them to celebrate their marriage with their close friends and family. She thought it would be a good *bonding* experience for us."

I didn't miss the way his eyes scanned down my body as he said *bonding* like he was thinking dirty thoughts.

"A reception?" The last thing I needed was to be forced to spend more time with Connor. I was feeling especially weak after my run-in with Peter, and I already knew I wasn't that strong where Connor was concerned. Just being in his presence now made my knees feel wobbly and my heart race.

He stepped closer, and my skin felt electrified from his nearness. His dark eyes turned heated, and that cocky smirk I should've hated, but didn't, appeared.

"Scared you won't be able to keep your hands off me?"

Yes.

"You wish," I said, but there was a tremor in my voice that gave away the truth.

"I do wish," he murmured. His eyes dropped down to my mouth, and I swore I stopped breathing. "I wish you couldn't stop thinking about me the way I can't stop thinking about you."

Wish granted. I hadn't stopped thinking about him since he was just an anonymous man who showed me, unlike anyone else, ways my body could fall apart in bliss.

His head dropped slowly down, bringing our faces closer together.

"What are you doing?" I whispered, my voice breathy. Our chests were touching now, and my panties were soaked.

What was the power this man held over me? And why did it have to be *him* and not someone I wasn't newly related to?

"I know the stepbrother thing bothers you," he said, his voice low. His gaze dropped down to where my nipples were hard points that not even my bra could hide. "Or does it turn you on?" He moved his mouth to my ear. "Does it make you wet to think about how naughty it is to take your new stepbrother's big, fat cock down your throat? Or for him to slam his hard cock inside that nice, tight little pussy of yours?"

A shiver skittered through my body and I closed my eyes. His words were my undoing.

And honestly, I was tired of being the good little girl everyone thought I was. Where had following the rules ever gotten me? Alone and unsure of my future.

But right here, right now, there was something—someone—I could have if I wanted.

And damn did I want him.

He pulled his head back at the same time I opened my eyes, and instead of questioning every thought in my head like I usually did, I followed my instincts. I surged up, my hand wrapping around the back of his neck and pulling his mouth to mine. He didn't fight it, and I caught the brief smirk before our lips slammed together. He groaned as I licked the seam of his lips and then dipped into his mouth when he parted them. His arms wrapped around my back, holding my body tight against his while he let me control the pace of the kiss.

But not for long.

"Make no mistake, darlin'. I will fuck you right here out in the open if you don't open that door and get us inside."

Another shiver slid down my spine and he chuckled. "An exhibitionist, huh? I'll keep that in mind."

"I've never done anything like that," I whispered, my inexperience making me vulnerable. Connor had already shoved me so far outside my sexual comfort zone it wasn't even funny.

His gaze narrowed slightly as he studied my face. I didn't know what he saw there, but his expression softened, making him look younger and more carefree—tender even.

He brushed my hair behind my ear. "Tell you what, anything—and I do mean *anything*—you want to try, I'm game. We'll explore anything sexual you've ever wanted to do."

"What if I don't know what that might be? What if I don't know what's even out there to try?"

Heat returned to his gaze as that cocky grin took over the bottom of his face. "I'll happily be your guide into all things kinky." He pulled me flush against his body again, his lips grazing my ear as he spoke. "I already know you like being called a dirty little slut, and when you come, your pussy squeezes me better than anything I've ever experienced."

"If it feels so good, then why are we standing outside when we could be inside with you teaching me more things I might like?"

His grin grew into a full-blown smile that had me starstruck, and then in a blink, he dipped down and lifted me up, throwing me over his shoulder like I was a sack of potatoes.

I had just enough time to make sure my coffee didn't spill out of my hand.

"Keys, Sugar," he rumbled, his voice taking on that deep timbre that had my lady bits tingling.

"In my purse."

He grabbed them and opened the door swiftly, making his way—all the while carrying me with ease—up the stairs to my apartment on the third floor.

"You know there's an elevator, right?"

"Too slow. And when I kiss you again, I don't plan to stop until you've come on my face, fingers, and cock. Not necessarily in that order. Didn't think you were ready for possibly getting caught in an elevator."

Why was he still talking when my brain had stopped at the whole coming on his face, fingers, and cock part?

He must've picked up on my stupor because he chuckled and smacked my ass right as we reached my door. He slowly lowered my feet back to the ground, making sure my body slid along every inch of his in the process.

Christ, this man was dangerous to my libido.

He opened the door with a quick efficiency I would've never had, not with my entire body vibrating with need.

Then we were inside and he was closing the door behind him, his gaze watching me like a hunter watching his prey.

"I should warn you; I'm done letting you run away from me after we have sex. I'm not going to stop fucking you until this is well and truly out of our systems. So if you don't want that, you need to tell me now."

I didn't say a word. Instead, I put my coffee down on the table by my door and then wrapped my arms around his neck and brushed his lips with mine. He let out a low groan that made my panties even slicker and skyrocketed my desire.

"One more warning," he murmured, his voice a low and seductive rumble. "I may never get enough."

I didn't believe that for a second. A man like him was probably used to having tons of women. I knew that someday he might not even think about our tryst.

But I would.

He didn't have to worry. I was done fighting this—done being the good, rule-following daughter. For once, I was taking what I wanted and right now, that was Connor.

Even if it was stupid and he had heartbreak written all over him.

When I still didn't say anything, but just stared up at

him, letting him see all the need and longing in my eyes, he lifted me up, wrapping my legs around his hips. His lips slammed down on mine, and we both let out a moan.

This man could kiss like no other. His mouth was sinful and delicious and everything I never knew I wanted or needed.

I whimpered when he pulled back, but I should've known he wasn't actually stopping. Instead, he twisted so my back rested on the closed door, and he started kissing down my neck. There was a feverish hunger as he worked his way down to my collarbone and then lower.

He groaned and then set me down, ripping my shirt up and over my head and then working my leggings down my legs. I stared down at him as he got down on his knees to pull off my shoes followed by my leggings.

He stared at my bare sex, his mouth slightly parted before his gaze met mine. "You're perfect, you know that?"

My heart slammed against my chest. "I'm far from perfect."

Something changed in his gaze, but I couldn't name it. He shook his head. "Trust me. You're perfect...or maybe just perfect for me." He said the last part so softly I wasn't sure I heard him right.

Or maybe I was just afraid that I *had* heard him right. This was supposed to be just sex. Really hot, fucking amazing sex. But still *just* sex.

"Fuck me, Connor," I said, my voice a little shaky—both from nerves and desire. I wasn't usually so bold during sex.

Whatever was in his gaze burned away as fierce heat replaced it.

"Careful what you ask for, darlin'."

Rule #6

IT'S JUST SEX

CONNOR

She looked down at me like she expected me to ravage her—and I would, but first, I had other plans.

I picked her back up and walked through her apartment until I found her bedroom and then tossed her on the bed, loving the squeal she made before she landed with a plop. Her mouth was popped open and her eyes wide with surprise. Fuck, the things I wanted to do to that mouth.

But not yet. Instead, I stayed where I was, although it took every effort not to lean over her and kiss that luscious mouth of hers.

"Make yourself come," I demanded.

She stilled, and I wished with every fiber of my being that I could read her mind to know what she was thinking right then. She swallowed thickly and then gave a minuscule nod, almost like she was psyching herself up. Then her tentative fingers were sliding down her stomach to that paradise between her legs.

She was already glistening with arousal, and her fingers slid easily over her pussy lips before she moved them to her clit. I watched her every movement like a hawk, my eyes bouncing from where her finger swirled over her clit to her face. It didn't take long to notice she was struggling. And then she started moaning and closed her eyes, but her body wasn't clenching like it did with me. She wasn't breathless and her moans sounded fake.

"Stop."

Her hand stilled immediately and her eyes snapped open. Mine narrowed. "Why are you faking it?"

Her face fell and my gut clenched. I hated the doubt that took over her eyes.

"I, uh...I've never done this before."

I arched a brow. "You've never masturbated?" I didn't believe that for a second.

"Not in front of someone else."

My chest puffed up, but I tried to tamp down the sheer thrill I felt at knowing I was another first for her. "You don't normally use your fingers, do you?"

She shook her head, but held my gaze instead of looking away like she usually did. That was good. It meant she was starting to trust me, and I was fucking dying for her trust.

"How do you normally do it?"

She nibbled her lip and then leaned over to her night-stand and pulled out a pink bulb that looked like a rose at the top. "I use this."

"Do it like you normally would. Pretend I'm not here if it helps."

"I like you watching," she said, her voice so soft I almost couldn't make out the words.

Almost.

The lust that shot through me at her words made me rock forward, and it was only with sheer will that I kept my feet planted and my gaze locked on her.

She turned on the rose vibrator and leaned back against the bed, getting more comfortable. Her free hand went to her breast where she tweaked a nipple while she placed the vibrator near her clit. I watched as she moved it closer to her clit, and her breaths grew shallow. Her nipple pebbled as she pulled and pinched it, her eyes hooded and her mouth parted as a stuttered moan slipped out.

Now that was more like it.

Her hips rocked as she kept the toy on her bundle of nerves. "Oh God," she moaned. "I'm so close."

My brows shot up. "Already?"

"Yes-s-s," she stuttered, her legs starting to tremble.

Damn, I'd definitely be using this toy on her in the future if it made her come this fast.

Her gaze caught on mine. "I want to watch you touch yourself too."

She didn't have to ask me twice. My cock was already a stone in my pants just from watching her. I loved her sounds—her real sounds, not the fake shit she was poorly attempting before—and watching her body writhe in pleasure.

I ripped off my shirt and tossed it on the floor and then unceremoniously pushed down and kicked off my pants and briefs, my hand already stroking my cock while I watched her play with herself. Her heavy-lidded eyes watched my every movement as her breathing started to come out in more staccato pants.

"Oh, fuck," she cried, tilting her head back. "Connor!"

She screamed my name as she came, her thighs closing

as her whole body shook from the pleasure of that little toy on her clit. The sight of her was all it took for me to lose my goddamn mind.

I was moving before my brain registered the action, my hand grabbing hers and pulling the toy away only to replace it with my mouth.

Christ, no woman should taste this good.

I let out a groan, wanting her to know what she did to me, how needy she fucking made me. Her fingers gripped my hair hard and the sting made my balls tighten. Keeping my mouth on her pussy, I moved my gaze up to her face to find her beautiful eyes already locked on me.

"That's so hot," she whispered, her cheeks flushing a dark rosy pink, whether from the admission or her orgasm, I wasn't sure.

Without stopping my ministrations with my mouth, I slid two fingers over her slick pussy lips and then dipped them inside. She was unbelievably tight, and clearly still sensitive from her orgasm based on the way her cunt fluttered around my fingers.

Her breathing picked up again, and a whimper escaped when I curled my fingers, hitting that spot that made her squirt last time.

"Connor," she choked out my name, panicking.

"Trust me," I murmured against her clit and kept my gaze locked on her as I pushed her body. I wanted her to cover me in it.

"I can't."

"You can," I rumbled, thrusting more vigorously. She was close; I could feel it.

Her mouth parted in an O and her eyes crossed slightly as her body stiffened and then she was screaming and convulsing as she gushed, covering my face and her bedsheets. I lapped it up like it was water, letting out a groan of pure desire as my cock stiffened to a painful degree.

Her orgasm went on longer than the last one, and I slowed my ministrations to slowly bring her back to earth.

She sagged against the bed, spent as the last of her tremors faded. "Shit," she whispered.

"Good shit?" I asked as I kissed my way up her body. She had a scar next to her belly button that I lingered on before making my way up to her mouth. I kissed her hard and she opened her mouth instantly, her tongue darting out to greet mine with an eagerness that had my stomach tightening.

This woman had no fucking clue how incredible she was.

But I did.

She was my shining light in the darkness I'd been living in. I didn't care if I knew I wasn't good enough for her; there was no way I could give her up.

"How'd you get that scar?" I mumbled against her lips. I knew she wanted this to be sex only, but I was already past that. I wanted to know everything about her and not just all the ways I could pleasure her body.

"From my appendectomy," she said, barely breaking the kiss, and then her hands were on my head, pulling my mouth to hers and making speech impossible.

I broke our kiss just long enough to dig a condom out of my pants pocket and cover myself before I slid into her slowly, savoring every inch of her tight heat wrapping around me.

"So goddamn perfect."

She rocked her hips, meeting me thrust for thrust, but shook her head. "You keep saying that."

It turned me on hearing how out of breath she was.

"Just the truth, darlin'." And because I knew she needed this to still just be sex, I leaned down so we were as close as two people could be and whispered against her lips, "Now keep being my perfect little slut and come on my cock. I want you to milk every drop of cum out of my balls with that perfect cunt."

Her eyes flared, but she couldn't deny she loved when I called her that. Her pussy didn't lie and it followed my orders to a T, tightening like a vise around my dick until she was screaming my name again and writhing underneath me. Her pussy milked my cock for all it was worth, and there was no way I could hold on any longer. With two more hard thrusts, I followed her over the edge, coming hard in the condom and wishing I was coming inside her bare. I shuddered and then dropped like a rock to the mattress next to her, completely spent. But not so spent that I didn't pull her body so she was nestled against mine.

Minutes passed as we both caught our breath and then I broke the silence.

"What changed your mind?"

I knew when I came here that she'd been set on us not continuing this thing, but there was a look in her eye when I saw her on the sidewalk outside her apartment that had been burned into my brain. Then when she didn't turn down my advances, I knew something had changed, and I'd been dying to know what caused it. Now as I lay here with her naked body snuggled against mine and my fingers twirling a strand of her hair, I couldn't hold the question back.

She stiffened slightly. "Does it really matter?"

It did to me. It'd never mattered with another woman before, but I knew from that first kiss that Jenna wasn't like the other women I'd been with in the past. She was special. After my experience overseas, I was painfully aware that life was too short to fight against what you really wanted.

And I wanted Jenna more than I'd ever wanted anything in my life. Just a few days and I already knew she was essential to my future happiness.

But she was also skittish. I didn't know why—yet—but I knew I had to play this carefully if I was going to win her over and make her as obsessed with me as I was with her.

"You seemed set on keeping us at a distance. I thought I'd have to work harder to convince you to give this another go."

She let out a resigned sigh and her body loosened up again. "Has anyone ever told you you're very stubborn?"

A laugh escaped, but despite what I knew she was attempting to do, she wasn't going to distract me from getting the answer I craved.

"Come on, Sugar, the suspense is killing me."

"I ran into my ex," she mumbled, and then it was my turn to stiffen. A million questions ran through my mind, but before I could pick one to ask, she kept going. "We've been broken up for two years, and I'm not in love with him or anything anymore, but seeing him was...the straw that broke the camel's back, I guess."

"What do you mean?"

"I thought this was just supposed to be sex."

"So, what? That means you can't tell me things?" It hadn't been just sex for me since the moment I walked into that restaurant and saw her sitting at the table with our parents, knowing I'd gotten a second chance for more than an epic one-night stand. But she wasn't ready to hear that.

"I've never done this before," she murmured. "I'm not

even sure what *this* is. Friends with benefits? Just scratching an itch?"

"Do you really want to label it, or do you just want to go with it and we make it whatever works for us?"

I knew what label I wanted, but that hadn't been included in either of the options she'd stated. Knowing where her head was at was both a blessing and a curse, but I needed her to open up to me.

I could already feel myself wanting to tell her things I'd never wanted to tell anyone before. Things I struggled even to tell the counselor the army had paired me up with before my discharge paperwork was finalized.

The three of us—the only survivors of a mission gone south—had been ordered to do mandatory counseling. I didn't know how well it worked for the other guys in my unit, but I knew my sessions had been unproductive as shit. The words hadn't come. But snuggled in bed with Jenna, I felt them rising to the surface. I wanted to talk. I wanted to bare my soul.

I wasn't sure what kind of witchcraft this woman had done to me, but I wasn't complaining, because holding her in my arms made me grateful I'd made it out alive. For the first time in months, I didn't want to drink my pain away.

I just wanted Jenna.

She chewed on her lip, thinking over my question, while I waited patiently for her to figure out what she wanted to do.

"I'm not where I thought I'd be," she whispered, her voice a little choked. "Things aren't going well for me at school. I barely passed last semester, and not for a lack of trying. Everyone in my class is doing internships this summer or taking extra classes, while my advisor encouraged me to take the summer off and reevaluate if this was the right path for me." She sniffled, and the way her voice cracked told me she was fighting back tears. "All I've ever wanted to do was work with animals. I have no backup plan. And then, I ran into Peter—my ex—and his wife. He's married, and even though I don't want him anymore, I feel like he's right where he always planned to be while my whole life is crumbling around me. My entire life, I've followed the rules and been the good girl, so for once, I wanted to say 'screw it' and try something different."

"And I'm something different?"

She huffed out a laugh, but there was no humor in it. "You're the opposite of everything. I've never done a hookup thing before. Peter was my first and..."

Her voice faded and I thought she was hoping I wouldn't put all those puzzle pieces together, but my tactical brain took every piece of information and came to the most logical conclusion.

"You've been celibate for two years?" There was no fucking way. Jenna was a smoke show. I mean, yeah, she hid it under conservative clothes, but her eyes drew me in and her mouth was like a siren's song that I wanted to drown in. Her curvy hips were the perfect grip when I was burying myself inside her. She was beautiful beyond measure.

She nibbled her lip. "Um, yeah."

"And this Peter guy was your first?"

"Yep."

I couldn't fight the smile spreading across my face. "So I'm only the second guy you've ever had sex with?"

She smacked my stomach. "You don't need to sound so giddy about it."

She had no idea. I was only the second man she'd been with, and clearly better than Peter based on some of the things she'd mumbled or screamed in the heat of the moment.

And if I had my way, it wouldn't matter that another man was her first because I'd be her last.

She squealed as I twisted, moving my body over hers, my once again hard cock resting at the apex of her glistening pussy and her thighs cradling my hips. Her eyes heated as her pelvis tipped up slightly.

"Did that turn you on?" she asked, a hint of disbelief in her voice.

"*You* turn me on."

And then I didn't let her say another word for a long time. I claimed her mouth the way I wanted to claim her heart. Twirling my tongue with hers, memorizing and savoring her flavor, kissing her lips until they were swollen. In between kisses, I grabbed another condom and slipped it on before gliding into her warm, wet heat.

Fuck, I could get lost in her body. I *wanted* to get lost—and found—with her.

I rocked my hips against hers, thrusting deep the way I'd already figured out that she liked. One hand slid into her hair, holding her head tight to my mouth while we kissed and fucked like I never had before.

There was no way this was just sex for her. It sure as shit wasn't for me. This wasn't like anything I'd ever felt. It was deep, raw, passionate, and tender.

As she started rocking her pelvis faster against mine and her mewls got louder, I slid my hand between us where my thumb rubbed tight circles over her swollen clit. She sucked in a sharp breath and then let out a loud moan that had my balls drawing up tight as she started convulsing around my cock. Her pussy gripped me so hard there was no way I could fight my own orgasm from ripping through me once again.

This woman was either going to break my heart or be my salvation.

I knew which one I was hoping for.

Rule #7

SAY WHAT'S ON YOUR MIND

JENNA

My jaw dropped as I looked up from where I was putting together the hamburger Uncle Wyatt had just made for me on the grill.

"What are you doing here?"

From my peripheral view I could see Uncle Wyatt look between me and the man standing in front of me, while my brain felt like it was on the fritz. Why the hell was Connor at my uncle's house? Uncle Wyatt hadn't spoken to my mom since my parents' divorce, so there was no way he'd just randomly invite over her current husband's son. And while Wyatt's barbecue parties were legendary—and the main reason I attended every chance I could—I doubted he would extend an invitation to someone he'd never met before.

Connor gave me his signature smirk and then his gaze moved to Wyatt and he reached out his hand. "Thanks for inviting me."

Wyatt put his metal spatula down and turned to

Connor, his gaze snapping between me and him while he took Connor's hand in a shake. "You know my niece?"

There was an undercurrent of threat in his tone, and I fought not to roll my eyes. Between him and my dad, I was lucky I ever dated at all. The overprotective buffoons practically scared every guy in my high school away from me.

"Wait, how do you two know each other?" I asked, my brow furrowed as I stared at them.

"Connor just started working for Carmichael Security."

I focused solely on Connor. "*That's* where you got your new job?"

How did I not know this? Could the world really be so small that my new stepbrother/hookup worked with my uncle?

"Now that we've cleared up how *we* know each other, which one of you wants to tell me how *you* know each other?" Wyatt asked, crossing his arms and staring both Connor and me down.

I opened my mouth to speak, but Connor beat me to the punch. "My dad just married her mom."

Uncle Wyatt's arms dropped as he shook his head. "Damn. Vanessa bagged another one already?" His attention focused on me. "Did she at least give you notice this time?"

I shrugged. "A day or two."

"Fucking hell," he murmured. Wyatt wasn't a fan of my mom, not just because of what she put my dad through when they were married, but also for how she constantly treated me. It wasn't really her fault. It was just the way she was. Like Connor had already figured out after only one interaction, my mom was self-centered, and I only seemed to matter when it was convenient for her.

I swallowed down the emotion that started to rise in my

throat. I normally had a pretty good handle on dealing with my mom and her shenanigans, but add her to the feeling of inadequacy I had because of vet school, and my emotions were running higher than usual.

"It's no big deal," I said, trying to move the conversation away from my mom.

"Well, I guess, welcome to the family for however long it lasts," Wyatt said with a pat to Connor's shoulder before he turned around and walked back to the grill, leaving Connor and me alone.

"So...Wyatt's your uncle?"

"Yep."

"Which would make Sadie..."

"My best friend," I finished for him.

He scratched his eyebrow. "I thought she was married to Wyatt's brother, Travis?"

"Travis is my dad."

"Right. So was she your best friend before or after she fucked your dad?"

I groaned and covered my face. "God, could you not?! I do not need that visual in my brain."

He chuckled, a deep, throaty sound that had my lady bits perking up. Goddammit. This man was turning me into a sex addict.

"Besides," I added, "You haven't seen them together. It took me a minute to get used to it, but their love is the kind people fight wars for and dream of having. They're lucky they found each other, even if it was unconventional."

He took a step closer and leaned down so his mouth was right next to my ear. "Seems you hooking up with your new stepbrother isn't the weirdest thing that's ever happened in this family."

God, he was right. When had my life turned into a soap opera?

"Wait, how do you know Sadie?"

"Grant. He's the buddy I'm staying with for the time being and he works with her. She hooked me up with Wyatt who got me an interview with Raf."

"Wow, it really is a small world."

"So, you gonna show me around the place?" he asked, smiling down at me.

My breath caught in my throat because this wasn't his usual cocky grin. This one was tender, and there was a simmering heat in his eyes that set both my heart and my panties ablaze.

No.

I would not catch feelings for him. This was sex. Plain and simple.

As if there was anything simple about sex, but still, I was determined to keep this as no strings as possible. My panties could burn up for all I cared, but my heart had to stay firmly out of the equation.

"Come on, I'll give you a tour and then we can eat."

His eyes lit up with that mischievous glint he always seemed to get when he was thinking about sex, and I smacked him on the chest while fighting back my own smile. I placed my plate down on the table, not sure if someone else at this shindig would snatch it up or not, but it didn't matter. I found myself more excited to give Connor a tour than to try and mingle with the other people here. It was both weird and exciting having him here at my uncle's house.

He waved to a few other coworkers—guys I'd met at previous get-togethers at my uncle's house—and then I took him inside and gave him the formal tour. I was about to head back out to the yard when he grabbed me right above my elbow.

"Walk me out through the front and around the side of the house."

"Why?"

"Because it looked like there were some fancy plants and shit and I wanna see it. Got a problem with that, darlin'?"

I huffed. "Fine."

We didn't talk as I walked out the front door with him close on my heels, then down the front porch stairs. I had just turned the corner down the long walkway that was covered with a pretty wooden trellis and grapevines which would lead us to the backyard when Connor grabbed my hand, spun me around, and planted a kiss on my lips.

I pushed against his chest and he let me pull away, both of us panting. "We can't kiss here," I hissed, glancing down the walkway, hoping we were far enough away no one would've happened to walk by right when he kissed me.

He pushed me back against the side of my uncle's house. "This walkway is at least forty feet, and everyone is down at the other end of the lawn. The risks are minimal as long as you're quiet." His eyes blazed with an intense level of desire that no man had ever given me before. From our very first encounter, he'd looked at me like this. He always saw all of me—all my desires, all my fears, all my vulnerabilities—even when I didn't want him to.

How did he do that?

We hadn't even known each other that long and yet the idea of taking this risk with him lit my whole body up like a bonfire. I glanced down the path. He was right. Most people were on the other end of the yard and wouldn't have reason to come down this way.

But I was still hesitant. The fact that my panties were soaked was a surefire sign that a part of me wanted to give it a try, but the exact location held me back.

I nibbled my lip, trying to find the nerve to tell him what I wanted when he put his fingers under my chin and tilted it up until I was forced to meet his gaze.

"You want to, don't you?" He smirked like he already knew the answer, which, of course, he did. "I bet you'd love it if I undid the buttons of your jeans and slid my hands into your panties. I bet you're already soaked for me, aren't you?"

My eyes flared, but I wouldn't give him the satisfaction of saying yes. Even if I wanted him to touch me like that, there's no way I could get into it here. Somehow the bar bathroom on that first night hadn't bothered me, but knowing my uncle, of all people, or one of his friends could catch me made my stomach curl with dread. I guess the good girl in me wasn't entirely banished.

His hand slid to the back of my neck even as his gaze seemed to burrow into mine. His touch was soft, and there was something in his eyes that had my heart racing.

"Connor," I said, my voice a hoarse whisper.

He leaned forward, his body barely brushing mine and our mouths almost touching. His gaze was fierce and his brown eyes swirled with an emotion I'd never seen on his face before. "You're a miracle, Jenna. Do you know that?"

I couldn't find my voice; it was trapped somewhere in my throat, blocked by all the emotion I was trying not to let spill out.

"My world was dark—pitch fucking black—until the minute you laid eyes on me in that bar." He snapped his lips shut like he was afraid of giving too much away, but he already had.

This wasn't just sex for him, was it? There was something more going on between us, even if I wanted to pretend there wasn't.

I was about to speak, although I honestly had no idea what words would tumble out of my mouth when laughter filtered through the window next to us—the open window. All it would take is one person getting closer to the window for us to be discovered.

I couldn't let my uncle find out this way. I hoped he'd never find out at all.

My eyes must've given away my panic because a look akin to pain and doubt crossed Connor's handsome face before he stepped back.

He gestured down the path that would lead us to the backyard. "After you."

I couldn't tell if it was disappointment in his voice or something else. A part of me wanted to ask, but a bigger part was too afraid of what his answer would be.

Whether he meant to or not, Connor had shifted the axis of this arrangement with his words, and I wasn't sure we would ever be able to go back to where we'd been before.

Rule #8

DON'T EYE FUCK YOUR NEW SUPERVISOR'S NIECE

CONNOR

I'd almost confessed. I'd almost told her I was falling—had fallen already—for her. But then I'd remembered why my world had been so dark before her, and all the words blew away like dust in the wind. I couldn't formulate my thoughts or push anything else. It's like the second I thought about the ambush and my life before my honorable discharge, every thought and feeling went on lockdown. Maybe it was a protective mechanism. I wasn't sure. All I knew was that Jenna was making me want more than I'd wanted in a very long time. She made me grateful I hadn't died that day.

At the same time, I was trying to come to grips with the way this woman had so quickly changed my life. This choke hold she had on me wasn't normal.

I wasn't a guy who got attached to women. I'd learned that lesson years ago when the one woman I put effort into ended up fucking another soldier. She didn't want me; she just wanted any soldier she could sink her claws into.

But I knew in my bones Jenna wasn't like any of the women I'd met in my life. She was loyal, strong, and fierce when she wanted to be. She owned me more with every breath she took. Voices in the backyard picked up the closer we got, and I heard her uncle calling for her.

What were the odds she was not only my new stepsister, but the niece of my new supervisor? Wyatt had seemed like a chill guy at work—a scary motherfucker when he wanted to be, but chill nonetheless—but he was as perceptive as I was and I knew he'd seen right through me when I showed up here and couldn't stop staring at Jenna. I knew I was going to get the third degree from him, but watching Jenna as she walked back, remembering the feel of her in my arms, the taste of her lips on mine, the way her eyes seemed to see in my very soul, made anything he could say or do to me one hundred percent worth it.

"So, that's the tour," she said loudly and I had to put my fist in front of my mouth to try to hide my grin. She was so obvious. We'd have to work on that.

"Connor." We both turned to see Wyatt's intense expression directed right at me. He didn't spare Jenna a glance as he walked toward us. "A word," he said and then kept on walking past me and into the house.

Jenna's eyes grew wide as panic filled her face, but I shook my head in a silent gesture that there was nothing to worry about and then followed her uncle into the house. He moved with purpose into a room off the side of the main hallway, and when I entered, it was clear this was his office.

"What's up?"

"Cut the shit," he said, spinning around and staring daggers at me that I'm sure would make a lesser man tremble, but didn't touch me. "What's going on with you and Jenna?"

I kept eye contact, something I'd learned in the army. Always look your superiors in the eyes, even if they have the upper hand. "I already told you. Her mom married my dad."

His eyes narrowed. "What else?"

I respected him as my supervisor, but like hell was I going to tell him what was really going on with me and Jenna. That was our business until she was ready to tell everyone.

I kept my mouth shut and watched his jaw twitch. "I swear to God, Connor, if you touch my niece, I'll fucking kill you and make it look like an accident."

"I have no doubt you could do that, but Jenna probably wouldn't appreciate it."

He leaned back on his desk, pretending to be relaxed and casual, but the tension in his shoulders gave him away. "And why is that?"

If he thought he was going to catch me in a lie, he was wrong. I hadn't lied about a single thing. Omissions didn't count. He was being nosy about something that was none of his business.

I shrugged and told him another truth, although this one was harder to admit because it was a weakness of Jenna's. "She seems to care what her mom thinks, and I doubt Vanessa would think highly of you killing her new stepson."

Wyatt's shoulders sagged slightly. "Fucking Vanessa," he murmured, so low I wasn't sure he intended for me to hear. Then his gaze was laser focused on me. "I don't believe you for a second, Connor. I think there is something going on, and I'm telling you right now, she's off-limits. You need to stay away from my niece, are we clear?"

"Crystal."

I understood him completely. I just had no intention of

following the law he'd laid down. Jenna might've been his to protect, but that was before. She was mine now.

We went back outside and Wyatt returned to his station at the grill while I immediately found Jenna sitting at a round table on the patio, sipping on what looked like lemonade. I detoured to the long table set up closer to the grill and made a plate of food, piling it high with as many options as I could find before joining Jenna.

She glanced up at me and then looked away, as if simply looking at me would give away the fact we'd seen each other naked. I ducked my chin to my chest, hoping it would hide the smile that was fighting to break free.

God, she was cute. She was sexy, beautiful, smart, and a million other things too, but right now she was fucking cute trying to hide the way she reacted to me. Even now, I could see the way her cheeks flushed pink and her breathing picked up. She could try to pretend to be unaffected by me, but she wasn't doing a very good job.

"What are you doing?" she asked, keeping her voice low even though there wasn't anyone around us. Most people were congregating by the pool or chatting with Wyatt by the grill. Some were in the house to escape the sun.

I gestured to my plate. "Eating." Then the left side of my mouth lifted. "And enjoying the view," I added, not hiding the way my gaze slid down her body and then back to her face.

She leaned forward, her voice low and bossy. "You can't look at me like that here," she hissed. "My uncle is right over there!"

I nodded. "So he is. But he's busy with his friends, and no one else is paying any attention to us anyway."

She inhaled deeply like she was trying to center herself from how taxing it was dealing with me, and I had to fight back my laugh. I couldn't remember the last time I'd felt as light as I did around Jenna.

But I could remember the last time I'd laughed before I met her, and that quickly had the smile slipping from my face. I pushed my plate closer to her. "Help yourself. I wasn't sure what you liked, so I got a little of everything."

She looked at my full plate and then back at my face before her delicate fingers darted out to grab a piece of watermelon.

I took a bite of my cheeseburger, enjoying the scenery and being near Jenna. Once I swallowed, I asked. "So, how come you're here?"

She looked at me like I was an idiot. "It's my uncle's house. I thought we already went over that."

"Yeah, but half these people are guys we work with or people who are his friends based on what I've gathered."

She leaned her elbow on the table and spun her body to face me. "And how did you figure that out when you've been following me around most of the time."

I tapped the side of my eye and then my ear. "The power of observation. I recognize the guys from the one full-staff meeting I attended, the others I caught bits of their conversations as you were giving me the tour and put the pieces together. But Wyatt's brother isn't here, or his wife—your best friend—so I guess I was just wondering what made you come to this thing."

Her cheek moved like she might be nibbling the inside of it. "My dad and Sadie were supposed to come today, but Sadie wasn't feeling well. I come often enough no one really questions it. I'm close to my dad and uncle, but my uncle works a lot so these types of events are really the only time I get to see him anymore, especially since I've been up in Sacramento for school the past two years."

"What made you want to become a veterinarian?" I pushed my plate a little closer, encouraging her to eat more. She grabbed some chips, eating them while her narrowed gaze looked at me accusingly.

"Why so many questions?" she asked.

I shrugged. "Just curious about you is all."

I wanted to learn all I could about her, and she'd proven to be more willing to share than I was considering what she'd already told me about her ex.

"I've always loved animals. My dad got me a dog when I was seven, and I loved her more than anything else. I named her Shadow because she'd follow me everywhere. I spent most of my childhood bouncing back and forth between my parents' houses, but my mom was off in Greece or France or something back then with one of her guys, so I was primarily with my dad. It was the happiest I'd been in forever. Then Shadow got sick. I was devastated. She wouldn't eat, wouldn't move. She'd look at me like she wanted me to save her, but I didn't know what was wrong. I felt helpless. We took her to the vet and they were able to diagnose the problem. She had Addison's disease which can be fatal if not managed. I remember the vet being so patient and calm, but also quick and focused. I was so scared, but she made the situation better. She eased my fears and taught us how to manage Shadow's Addison's. She saved my dog and unknowingly made me fall in love with a career I'd never really thought about." She laughed and the way her whole face lit up made me forget to breathe. "I think my dad thought I was just going through a phase like kids do when they say they want to be an astronaut or a racecar driver, but over the years, it never went away." Her smile dimmed, but it was her eyes that gave away the heartbreak she was trying to hide. "It's the only thing I've ever wanted to do."

Before I could ask her why she got sad all of a sudden, Wyatt came over with his own plate and a second with another cheeseburger that he placed in front of Jenna. He gave me a long look, and I knew my time alone with Jenna was over.

He didn't need to know I planned to go home with her tonight, and every night she'd let me.

Rule #9

GOOD FOOD IS ALL YOU NEED

JENNA

Talking about why I'd wanted to become a vet had unleashed a need in me that I could no longer ignore. So, two days later, I went into a local animal shelter and signed up to volunteer for the remainder of the summer. I'd volunteered here before when I was in high school so there wasn't much I needed to do except update my mailing address and learn some of the new systems they'd put in place since I was last here.

Being surrounded by animals was both a gift and a curse. It reminded me of why I'd wanted to be a veterinarian in the first place, but it was also painful to leave at the end of the day. I wanted to adopt them all and take them home with me.

But I couldn't deny that I was in a better mood than I'd been in days as I walked up to my apartment, a smile on my face that had been there most of the day. It was a good feeling.

When I arrived at the top of the stairs, my steps faltered

because Connor was standing at my door, four brown paper bags at his crossed feet as he waited patiently for me.

"Hey," I said, pulling my keys out of my pocket and unlocking the door. "I hope you haven't been waiting long. I didn't realize you were coming by tonight."

He shrugged and smiled as if nothing bothered him, but I knew that wasn't true. Every so often when we were together, he'd get a distant look in his eyes and then search me out. I wasn't sure he was even aware of it.

"I figured we could make dinner and hang out," he said, picking up the bags as if they weighed nothing and following me into my apartment.

I dropped my keys on the counter and then looked through the bags as he placed them down next to my keys.

I started pulling out the groceries one by one. "What is all this?"

"This," he said, taking the onion out of my hand, "is everything I need for my grandma's famous chicken pot pie. It's a classic, and if you say you don't like chicken pot pie, I'm going to have to call you a liar."

I couldn't help but laugh at how serious his tone was. "I do, in fact, enjoy a good chicken pot pie. Although that's not something I expected you to know how to make."

"I'm a man of many talents," he said with a wink.

He started prepping everything and I watched, mildly amused and also insanely turned on. I'd never had a guy cook for me before and I had to admit it was hot.

"Is there something I can help with?"

"Nope," he said, a carefree grin on his face that had my heart racing faster. "Just sit there on the counter and keep me company while I make you the best dinner of your life."

"Those are big words. Setting the bar pretty high there."

"I stand by my statement. Just you wait, Sugar."

My whole body nearly melted into a pile of swoon on the counter. Damn, I was such a sucker when he called me Sugar. He paused long enough to pull his phone out and fiddle with it before music came through its speaker. He turned down the volume enough so we could still talk or let it be ambient noise.

Personally, I didn't mind just sitting here watching him work with such precision. I never felt like I had to be "on" when I was with Connor. I never needed to fill any silence or second-guess myself like I did so frequently these days with other people. Connor made me feel safe to just be. It was something about his demeanor and the way he also seemed relaxed as soon as he walked in my door.

As he moved around my kitchen with ease, I started to get curious. "Did your grandma teach you this recipe or your mom?"

He laughed a full belly laugh that made a smile pull at my cheeks. "My mom can't cook to save her life. Thanks to my dad's money, she was always able to hire help. My grandma taught me one summer when I stayed with her."

"Why did you stay with her? How old were you?"

I had a million questions. This was the most he'd told me about his past. Neither of us tended to talk much about that, but there were little things about his personality and character that I'd learned over the last couple of weeks that made me want to know everything about him.

He glanced up at me before focusing back on the dish. His Adam's apple bobbed as he swallowed, and I wondered if he was going to pretend I'd never asked. Disappointment started to filter through the contentment I'd been feeling when he cleared his throat.

"My parents' divorce was nasty, so they shipped me off to my only other living relative. I spent that summer in

Oklahoma with my grandma. The divorce was just an excuse that time since they usually shipped me off to her at some point throughout the year. Whenever they were too busy, which was pretty much any time I wasn't in school." He smiled at me, but it belied the weight of the memory that was clear in his eyes. "I think my grandma only taught me so I wouldn't get into trouble since I'd just turned twelve and discovered girls did not in fact have cooties."

I laughed at that. I could absolutely see him as a cute twelve-year-old boy flirting with every girl and woman he met.

Since he was opening up, I decided to push my luck and ask him something else I was curious about—although it was hard to pick only one thing.

"What do you do for fun?" Since I'd met him, he'd spent pretty much all his free time with me.

He shrugged. "Work out. Fuck you," he said with a saucy smile that made me roll my eyes.

"I'm serious," I said.

He waggled his eyebrows. "So am I."

"I don't really know anything about you."

He hummed but didn't really respond as he finished making the pot pie and then put it in the oven. When he closed the oven door, he walked over to me, fitting his body in between my legs and placing his hands on either side of my hips. His dark gaze held me captive, and I wished I knew every thought that went through his head.

"You know the things that matter," he said, his voice low.

I frowned. I didn't think that was true. Our past mattered—the things that made us the people we were—and I could no longer deny that I was curious about his.

He leaned closer. "You know that I will always show up

when you call." He leaned to the side, pressing a kiss to my neck. "You know I will always make you come first." He moved to the other side, kissing me there too. "You know you'll never starve when I'm around—for food or orgasms." He kissed my lips. "You *know* who I am. All the other stuff is just extra."

The other stuff was important to me. I tried to hide my disappointment, but I knew I wasn't succeeding when he grabbed my hands and pulled me off the counter. He surprised me when he pulled me into his arms, wrapping one arm around my lower back while the other held my hand. His gaze remained on mine as he started moving us around the kitchen, gently swaying our bodies to the soft music playing from his phone.

My body softened against him, and I let our movements wash away my frustration that he never seemed to let me in. We danced like that through the end of the next song, and then a classic from old middle school dances came on and we both burst into laughter. He spun me in circles in my kitchen while we waited for dinner to cook and when it was done, I set the table while he set his masterpiece in the center.

We sat next to each other and he watched me take my first bite. He arched a brow, waiting for my reaction, and I hated to do it but there was no way I could lie.

"Okay, you win. This is the best chicken pot pie I've ever had."

His smile grew, and for a second it was hard to breathe. This man was so dangerous to my heart because watching his face light up made me want to watch it happen every night.

Rule #10

TIES SHOULD ONLY BE WORN AROUND YOUR NECK

CONNOR

"You were out late."

I looked up from where I was sitting on Grant's couch, drinking coffee while I scrolled mindlessly on my phone.

"Didn't realize I had a curfew, Mom."

Grant shook his head. "Fucker," he mumbled. "So, who is she?"

"Who are you talking about?" I asked, looking back down at my phone and pretending like I had no idea what he was referring to.

"Alright, I get it. She's secret sex for now, but you'll tell me eventually. We're best friends. We basically tell each other everything."

Not everything.

We used to, but then I went overseas, and the life I knew got blown to pieces. I hadn't told him the truth about what happened over there, and like a good friend, he hadn't pushed. I knew that conversation would come sooner or later, but it wasn't one I was ready to have now.

And I sure as shit wasn't ready to talk about Jenna.

"How are things going at Carmichael Security?" he asked.

Carmichael Security was an elite security firm here in LA. As soon as the owner, Raf, had heard about the military operations I was a part of, he'd hired me on the spot. All he needed was my DD-214 to ensure that I was in fact honorably discharged and wasn't lying about my military background. I also had to pass a psych eval and thorough background check. He was allowing me to work on a probationary period until those things were checked off, which meant I was always working with a supervisor instead of solo. I still couldn't get over the fact my supervisor was Jenna's uncle.

"So far, so good." The pay was good and the work was easy compared to what I was used to.

"Are you excited about it?" Grant asked.

I finished my coffee and then set my empty mug down on the end table. "I don't know. I never really planned for life after the military."

I didn't think there would *be* life after the military. I planned to stay in until death or retirement, but I took those options off the table after the ambush. I couldn't do it any longer. Maybe that made me weak, but I couldn't get out of the army fast enough after that shitshow overseas. The problem was, I wasn't good at much else, so doing bodyguard work made the most amount of sense.

"How are you doing with all that? We haven't really had a chance to talk."

I tilted my head and offered him a smirk. "Yeah, well, you know I've never been a big talker."

It was true. Growing up with two parents who had passive-aggressive down to a T, I'd learned to keep my shit locked down and mind my own business. They rarely talked to me, and I rarely talked to them. The only person I'd ever confided in was Grant, but there were some things I could no longer share with him. I didn't know if I'd ever be able to. Hell, I wasn't sure I'd be able to share them with anyone.

Jenna was the first person I'd wanted to share them with, but the thought alone of letting the words spill free was enough for them to get locked in my throat.

Maybe that mission had fucked me up worse than I realized.

He frowned. "I hope you're talking to someone at least. Are you still seeing that therapist?"

He was going to keep pushing if I didn't shut this down, and clearly he wasn't taking the hint, which meant it was time to change the direction of our conversation, and there was one topic I knew for certain Grant couldn't stop talking about. "So, how are things going with your boss?" I asked, quickly changing the subject.

His frown morphed to disappointment before he cleared his throat and looked down at the coffee table between us. "There's a rumor going around she's getting divorced."

Well, now that was interesting.

Grant had been secretly in love with his boss, Shannon Perry, since the moment he met her. But she'd been married even then and he was not the kind of guy to poach another man's woman. So he dated women who clearly did nothing for him, while he pined for the woman he saw day in and day out. I was pretty sure Grant had made a careful study of Shannon over the two years he'd worked for her.

"You think it's true?"

He slanted his gaze at me. "Does it make me an awful person if I hope it is?"

"Absolutely."

He threw a napkin at me, but my comment did the trick and a small smile lifted his lips. "How could he be dumb enough to let her go? I mean, she's fucking incredible. She—"

"Yeah, yeah, I've heard the speech about how amazing she is, starting this company from the ground up and yada yada yada. Get to the good stuff. Are you going to find out if it's true so you can make your move?"

He hesitated only briefly and then his smile grew like the Grinch who stole Christmas. "I mean, if he's going to be dumb enough to let her go, I'm going to be smart enough to make her mine."

"Atta boy."

I fucking hated ties. They made me feel like I was being choked by an article of clothing, and loosening them never seemed to help. I didn't have to wear them for every job, but most of the time I did. It was so far the biggest complaint I had about my job, but Raf was a stickler about looking professional.

But then Jenna's door swung open and her gaze devoured me in my suit. Maybe ties weren't that bad after all if this was the reaction I got.

There were no words exchanged before she pounced on me like a starving lion, her arms around my neck and her thighs snug against my hips as she locked her ankles at my lower back. I gripped her ass and took her lips in a savage kiss as I walked her back into her apartment and slammed the door closed with my foot.

The bed was too far away, but the kitchen table would do.

Her hands were in my hair, her pelvis rocking back and forth on my already achingly hard dick.

Fuck, she had me so worked up, I wasn't going to last long if she kept this up, and I had plans for her body. That's when I realized how useful my tie could be, and my opinions about ties changed completely.

I loosened the tie just enough to get it over my head then grabbed both of Jenna's hands, putting the loop around them before pulling it tight. She stared at me wide-eyed and beautiful, her breasts pushing against her shirt and jiggling from her shallow breaths.

"Be a good girl and lie back for me, Sugar." With a shaky inhale, she did as I asked. "Now put those hands over your head." Her submission as she once again quickly did what I asked made my desire for her stroke up my spine until I felt like it was squeezing my heart and my dick at the same time.

Fuck, she really was perfect for me. I'd never met anyone so responsive and willing to try new things. But it was more than that. She had a gentleness that softened all my rough edges, that calmed me when the storm in my mind would rage. After a long day, being near her felt like the greatest relief as a sense of peace I never thought I'd feel again wrapped around me.

"You're such a good girl," I murmured, leaning over her until my lips brushed hers faintly. "I bet that sweet pussy is already soaked for me, isn't it?"

A soft whimper escaped as her body shuddered on the table.

It was so hot that she got turned on by dirty words. And it worked out for me since it turned me the fuck on too.

I kissed her lips, sliding my tongue across the seam until she parted them before slanting my mouth more firmly on hers and plunging my tongue inside to tangle with her own.

I let out a groan when her body arched up to touch me while her mouth met mine stroke for stroke. God, this woman could kiss. I couldn't wait to feel her mouth on my cock again, but first I had to taste her. I'd been craving it all damn day.

I broke our kiss but nearly kissed her again when she let out a little mewl in protest.

"Hold that thought, darlin'," I murmured as I made my way down her neck to her collarbone. I moved her shirt up her stomach and over her breasts, then her head before I let it hang on her wrists where they were still tied together above her head. She was wearing yoga pants that slid off like butter down her legs, taking her thong underwear with them.

And then she was laid out gloriously naked on the table like a feast.

"Fuck, you have no idea how sexy you look right now."

Her mouth was parted and her eyes hooded, but it was her hard nipples pointing straight up at the ceiling that snagged my attention. Leaning down, I sucked on a stiff tip, eliciting a moan from her. Moving to her other breast, I repeated the teasing suck while my hand slid up her leg and then over the arousal dripping from her soaked pussy. She sighed as my finger circled her swollen clit.

"That feels so g-good," she stuttered as her pelvis thrust up, seeking more friction.

"Have I told you," I murmured against her skin while I once again worked my way down her body, "that I love how responsive you are?"

Her cheeks flushed pink, and not just from arousal.

"Your asshole ex never told you that, did he?" I asked.

She shook her head, and I narrowed my eyes. I wanted her words, to hear her soft melodic voice filling the air around me. I hated that he'd planted all sorts of bullshit doubts in her head.

"I want you to do something for me."

"What's that?" she asked.

"I want you to forget everything that fucker ever told you about your body, because he clearly didn't know jack shit."

Her lips tilted up as a smile spread across her face, and the light in her eyes that I was falling for more every second shone brighter than the sun.

"Make me forget." Her eyes sparked with the challenge, and no way was I going to let it go.

But I decided to let my actions do the talking.

I spread her thighs wide, my mouth watering at the sight of her exposed pink pussy that practically glittered in the light from her arousal. Dipping my head down, I took a long lick from her pussy lips to her clit. Her thighs clenched, her legs trying to close in on my head, but I was prepared for her body's response and held her legs open with my hands.

Another lick and I had to close my eyes as my cock pulsed with need in my pants. Her taste exploded on my tongue—musky and tangy and delicious. I could eat this woman all day every day. But I wanted to see her body explode from pleasure. I wanted to pump every ounce of pleasure out of her until she was limp and content on the table.

She was my feast and fuck, was I starving.

Holding her thighs firm, I teased her with my tongue, dipping it into her pussy and pulling it out, mimicking what I planned to do with my finger. Then I moved my mouth to her clit, forming a suction around it and then flicking it with my tongue. She moaned as her back arched on the table and my gut tightened with want. I needed to make her come soon, or I would lose my resolve to give her two orgasms before I buried my cock inside her.

I alternated sucking and flicking her clit until she was thrashing on the table, her cries of pleasure music to my goddamn ears. And then she sucked in a sharp breath, and her whole body tensed before shuddering as her hips rocked against my mouth and her release flooded my taste buds.

"Oh my God," she panted as she started to come down, but I wasn't done yet.

I slid one finger inside her, taking her by surprise but watching her face for any signs of distress or discomfort. Instead that hooded gaze locked on mine and she nodded.

"Make me come again."

I smirked. Her wish was my command.

I pulled my finger out and pushed two in on the next thrust. "Oh fuck," she moaned, her arms rising on the table as if she was about to bring them down to bury them in my hair.

"Keep those hands above your head, Sugar, or all this stops."

She let out a small groan of frustration, but put her arms back above her head. "Good girl," I murmured right as I thrust three fingers inside her. I didn't go slow this time—my patience was too thin as it was—instead I thrust in and out rapidly, aiming for that spot I knew would cause her to gush all over me.

Some men hated squirting—some women too—but not me. I loved watching a woman come so hard she released a torrent of fluid everywhere. I loved even more that no one else had ever made Jenna come this hard.

This seismic pleasure was all mine.

"Oh my God, oh my God," she started murmuring, her breaths coming faster and her legs tensing up.

"No God here today, darlin', just me." And then I picked up my pace and within three thrusts, she went off like a bomb, screaming as her release tore through her and wet the front of my pants.

"Fuck, you're so goddamn beautiful," I whispered as I leaned over her nearly spent body and kissed her hard. Her arms wrapped around my neck, and I allowed it because honestly, I craved her affection. I was desperate for her to want me as badly as I wanted her all the fucking time.

"You're so good at that," she panted, and my smirk reappeared, pride dripping from every pore.

"Think you can come for me one more time?"

She blinked up at me and then that luminescent smile broke out over her face and sucked all the air from my lungs.

Would there ever come a day when I didn't fall harder every second for this woman? She'd come out of fucking nowhere and already owned me completely, which would be terrifying if I wasn't so gone for her.

"I think you'll help me get there," she said as she lifted her lips to mine for another kiss.

"You're damn right I will," I said, pulling back so I could take off my shirt and pants. I unbuttoned my white shirt slowly, loving the way her eyes sparked with desire as I exposed each inch of skin. I dropped it to the floor to join her clothes and then undid my belt buckle and slowly slid it out of each loop.

Maybe next time I'd see if she was into light spankings with a belt. It wasn't my thing necessarily, but I knew she wanted to explore when it came to sex, and I was nothing if not accommodating when it came to her wants and desires.

I kicked off my shoes and pulled off my socks, then my pants were gone next. With one push, my boxer briefs followed, and then I was completely bared to her. I gripped my cock in my hand, squeezing it and stroking slowly, if just to remind it to calm down because I still had to make her come one more time before it was our turn.

She was no longer looking at my face, but staring hard at my erection, her eyes wide. "I still can't believe that thing fits in me. It's huge."

My dick twitched and her gaze shot to mine. "Careful, Sugar, it turns me on to hear you talk so highly of my cock."

She smiled and then let out a light little laugh that had my heart beating double time. I wanted to make her laugh again. Hell, she should laugh like that every day.

"Come here and fuck me already," she said as her laugh died away and the room grew quiet again.

I didn't need to be told twice. I snagged a condom out of my pants pocket and rolled it on and then in one smooth motion, I was back between her gorgeous thighs, rubbing the head of my dick over her clit. Her hips tilted up, and I accepted the invitation, pushing my thick cock into her, relishing in the snug fit.

I tried to hold myself back from the desire pounding in my skull to thrust all the way into her. I didn't want to hurt her, especially as tight she was.

"Goddamn it, Jenna," I choked, my body fighting against my mental restraints, desperate to be buried inside her. "You feel so fucking good."

"Right back at ya," she murmured before letting out a blissful moan as I slid the final few inches. My pelvis rubbed against her clit and she let out a shuddery breath.

"So good," she panted.

I needed her lips again before I made her shatter underneath me, so I leaned over and took her mouth in a fierce kiss. Her tongue slid against mine, meeting my eagerness and then some. My hips rocked out slightly and then back in, and we both groaned at the heavenly sensation.

There was no better feeling in the world than being balls deep inside Jenna. Not a single fucking one.

My restraint was running thin, and my thrusts started coming faster and harder, her moans only spurring me on until any control I had completely snapped and I was pounding into her like our lives depended on it. Her hands turned to grip the table above her head, the tie still wrapped around her wrists and her legs locked around my hips. I gripped her hips and canted them ever so slightly to hit her at a better angle, and she let out a scream as her pussy squeezed me so tight, it nearly took me to my knees.

"Fuck," I growled, trying to hold off just a little longer, but it was no use. She felt too good and I was too needy for her. With one more thrust, I let out my own shout as my release ripped through me.

When I'd caught my breath, I looked up and found Jenna smiling at me, her cheeks rosy with a post-orgasmic glow and her eyes shining bright. It was that moment when it hit me hard—I was going to marry this woman.

Rule #11

TELL YOUR BEST FRIEND
EVERYTHING

JENNA

There was only one person I was going to call when it came to planning my mother's reception and that was Sadie. That girl could plan like nobody's business, and she had an eye for decoration that always left me amazed. It was no wonder she was so good at her job as an interior decorator. She had been good at it from an early age, always enjoying turning a blank, boring space into something that fit exactly what you were looking for whether it was comforting, inviting, modern, classic, vintage, unique. You named it and she could completely make it come to life.

But I also wasn't surprised to see her look at me like I was crazy when she showed up to the space—the very expensive space—my mom had picked out.

"You've got to be kidding me," she said.

"'Fraid not."

"Your mom picked one of the most expensive venues in the city for a reception to celebrate a marriage that probably won't last longer than the salad in my fridge?"

"Yup."

She shook her head as she stared around the space—a fancy ballroom with beautiful crystal chandeliers and gold filigree around all the accents on the walls and window trim.

"What a waste." Then she firmed up her shoulders. "Alright, let's turn this into the best reception of her damn life and hope she actually appreciates it. Did she give you any other guidelines?"

I was hoping I could stall her before she asked that question.

My mom dropped off an entire binder full of things she wanted, but I'd left it at home and Connor was bringing it. Despite Sadie being my best friend in the whole world, I hadn't told her about Connor yet. Not all the nitty-gritty details at least. She knew he was my new stepbrother and we were planning this together, but that was about it. I had accepted her relationship with my dad, but sometimes it still felt weird to share details about my sex life. I didn't think she'd tell him, but I also didn't want her to have to lie to her husband.

It put me in an awkward spot.

"I come bearing gifts." Connor's deep voice penetrated the silence that had filled the room when I'd frozen at Sadie's question.

She turned toward the door, and I didn't miss the way her eyes widened and then the small wink she shot me when Connor walked past us to the table so he could set down the giant binder.

"You must be Connor," she said, putting out her hand for a shake. "Sadie," she said when he grabbed it.

"Nice to meet you," he said and then his dark gaze turned to me. "Jenna."

The way my name rolled off his tongue sent a shot of lust straight through my body. He said it the way he did when he was thrusting inside me and holding me right on the edge of release. My cheeks flushed and I swallowed thickly. "Connor."

That arrogant little smirk that both annoyed and aroused me appeared on his face.

Sadie's eyes narrowed as her gaze bounced between us, and she tilted her head to the side ever so slightly. I knew her well enough to know the wheels in her brain were turning, and I did not need her to pick up on the sexual tension between Connor and me while we were supposed to be planning this doomed reception.

"So, should we sit down? We've only got two weeks to get this thing finished," I said.

Sadie's eyes practically popped out of her head. "Two weeks?! Jesus, your mom really loves to screw with people's schedules. I can't even believe she got this place on such short notice."

"There was a cancellation," Connor told her, "or else she would've been out of luck."

Sadie's eyes turned sympathetic as she focused on me. "Does she even realize the pressure she's putting on you? I know professional event coordinators who would struggle with something like this, and they thrive on the pressure of pulling off awesome events in a blink."

"It's fine," I said.

"It's not," Connor said, matter-of-factly. "Jenna's mom is kind of a selfish diva, which means she's exactly my dad's type. She'll get what she gets." He nodded at the binder. "She can fill three of those things with details of what she wants. Doesn't mean she's getting it. Jenna's not bending over backward to make this happen, and neither am I. It can be nice and simple and they can both be grateful they didn't have to lift a finger. It's supposed to be about the marriage, not showing off."

Sadie and I both stared at Connor, our jaws dropped and eyes wide. Sadie recovered faster than I did. "Have you met Vanessa? It's always about showing off and never about the marriage."

"That doesn't change the fact that Jenna's not overdoing it for her mom who won't appreciate her taking on that level of stress anyway."

He held Sadie's gaze like he was daring her to question him. A lump formed in my throat as I stared at him in wonder. The feminist in me once again was saying I should be pissed that he was speaking for me, but I'd never had anyone that wasn't my dad, uncle, or Sadie defend me against my mom. Peter never bothered to get involved, and barely noticed when I was frustrated or hurt by my mom's actions and the way she treated me like either a trophy or a servant, but never a daughter.

"Alright, well, let's take a peek at this binder and see what's even feasible. I don't want to give Vanessa any ammo to guilt trip Jenna for anything." Sadie pulled the binder closer and opened it, but my gaze was still focused on Connor, who finally looked at me.

That lump in my throat grew as my heart swelled at the tenderness in his gaze—the care and protection barely hidden under the surface. No one had ever looked at me like this. No one had ever *seen* me the way he did.

The way he looked at me every time we were in the same room.

He scooted his chair closer so he could look over the binder with Sadie, but it also brought him closer to me, and he put his hand on my thigh under the table where Sadie wouldn't see. He gave it one little squeeze and he might as well have been squeezing my heart.

My body was having an internal freak-out—my heart swelling with an emotion I refused to acknowledge after such a short amount of time, my stomach in knots with what this meant, and my stupid vagina wet for him already at his mere presence.

Sadie started talking and I tried to focus, but I was way too distracted. Connor was too close and he smelled too good and every time he looked over at me, there was that tenderness in his gaze that felt like so much more than "just sex."

I stood up abruptly. "Uh, I need to go to the bathroom."

Sadie looked at me like I was a weirdo for announcing it to the room, and Connor grinned like he knew I was freaking out. But he shouldn't have been able to read me that well. We'd only known each other a few weeks, for fuck's sake.

I dashed off to the bathroom and splashed some water on my face. I stared at my reflection in the mirror—my flushed cheeks, my frantic eyes, my bottom lip which had a slight indent from where I'd been nibbling it too much.

"What is wrong with me?" I whispered to my reflection. "Why can't I do no-strings-attached sex? Why does my stupid heart have to get involved?" I was actively whisper-chastising myself. I shoved my fingers in my hair. "God, I'm really losing it."

The door opened and Sadie walked in, her perfectly manicured brow arched and her arms crossed. "So, how long were you going to wait to tell me that you're hooking up with your new stepbrother?"

My eyes bugged out. "He told you?!"

Her smile turned victorious. "Nope. But you just confirmed what I suspected."

Damnit.

"It's not like that," I said.

"Sure, it's not." She walked over to the mirror and fixed her hair which didn't really need fixing in the first place. "But riddle me this. If it's nothing, why do you look like you just ran away from your grade school crush after saying something embarrassing?"

"I do not look like that."

She cocked her head to the side in a gesture that shouted *you really want to play it that way with me.*

My shoulders dropped and I leaned against the sink, my back now to the mirror. This was my best friend. If I couldn't tell her, who could I tell?

"I had a one-night stand."

"What?!"

I held my hand up. "Not even close to the part you'll be shocked about. Anyway, I had a one-night stand with some guy I met at a bar, and then the next day I showed up for brunch with my mom and he was there."

"Connor?"

"Yep. My new stepbrother who also happened to be the man who'd just blown my mind the night before."

Her jaw dropped. "Nooo."

"Yep."

"Holy shit."

"My thoughts exactly. Then I ran into Peter, who's married by the way."

"His poor wife," she said like the good friend she was and made me smile.

"Anyway, Connor came over after that run-in to discuss organizing this party, and I decided I was sick of always being a good girl who follows the rules and that a little hookup might be good for me. Now here we are."

I could feel her staring at the side of my head so I finally faced her. "What?"

"But it's more than sex now, isn't it?"

"Why do you think that?" I asked, genuinely curious. Sadie was more perceptive than most, but if she was picking up on it, were we being more obvious than we should be? Was *I* being too obvious about my conflicted feelings?

"Because he watched your every move the moment he entered the room. Maybe not with his gaze, but it was obvious he was very aware of where you always were in relation to him. Plus..."

She nibbled her bottom lip and looked over at the closed bathroom door.

"Plus what?" I asked.

She turned back to me and her gaze was softer. "He looks at you like Travis looks at me."

I parted my lips to deny it but then sagged back against the sink. Oh my God. *That* was the look he gave me, the look I couldn't quite place but made me feel warm and fuzzy and wanted.

"We should get back out there," I said vacantly and then left the bathroom. I didn't wait for her to follow, but I didn't need to; she was right on my heels.

I walked into the ballroom and Connor looked up from the binder, his gaze finding mine instantly. His shoulders dropped slightly, almost like he was relieved, but that wasn't what had all the breath trapped in my lungs and my heart beating so fast it could compete with a hummingbird's wings.

He looked at me like I was his.

And that ache in my chest told me that's exactly what I was.

But was it even possible for a man like Connor to ever really be mine? Or was I doomed for heartbreak all over again?

Rule #12

SEX SOLVES EVERYTHING

JENNA

Today was a really bad day.

A friend of mine from my veterinary program was down in LA for the weekend and wanted to hang out before she had to head back up north. We'd grown close last semester, but as she yammered on and on about her internship and how well she ended up doing in the class we both struggled with, my insides shriveled.

Why did everyone else seem to be doing so well in our program while I was drowning? Was I really not cut out to be a veterinarian?

My heart ached as I let myself into my apartment and then dropped my keys on the table by the door. I stood there, staring at the apartment that was only mine temporarily and then sagged against the door before sliding to the floor. I wrapped my arms tight around my bent knees and finally let out the emotion I'd been holding in ever since Sara started talking about how awesome her internship was going and how she'd learned so much, yada, yada, yada.

Tears cascaded down my face as I was forced to confront reality. All I'd ever wanted to do was be a veterinarian—to work with animals. But maybe it was time to face facts that I wasn't good enough. I was falling behind my peers, more with every day that passed. I shouldn't have listened to my advisor. I should've gotten my own internship to prove her wrong.

Why didn't I argue against her suggestion?

Why?

I leaned my head back against the door, feeling the tear tracks running down my face, but I lacked energy to wipe them away. There was no one here anyway.

And then, right on cue, someone knocked on the door. Could I really not be left alone to wallow in my misery for five freaking minutes?

I pushed myself up to standing and wiped any sign of tears away. I could only hope my eyes weren't too red-rimmed. I looked through the peephole and my stomach clenched for a whole new reason.

It wasn't just anyone on the other side of the door. It was Connor. I should've known; we hadn't spent a night apart since our meeting with Sadie over a week ago. I thought I'd done a good job of keeping my growing feelings hidden from him, but that was easy since we were mostly busy having a lot of sex.

He knocked again and I knew I needed to open the door, but if anyone would catch on to my emotional state, it was likely him. Every time he came over, his gaze would sweep over my face like he was cataloging every inch.

I opened the door and the smell of my favorite takeout—something I'd shared with him last week—wafted up from a brown paper bag in his hand. My stomach grumbled. "Did you bring dinner?"

"What's wrong?" he asked, his voice gruff as he ignored my question. He remained standing in the hall, his broody gaze locked on my face as if staring hard enough would tell him all he needed to know without me whispering a word.

I shrugged. "Just a bad day." I tried to feign a smile. "But it's better now as long as there are potstickers in that bag you're holding."

"They're your favorite." He remembered.

"They are," I said thickly, whatever smile I had mustered disappearing like it had been swept out to sea.

He paid attention to my favorites. He held me every night. He showed up. Hell, how many times had I wished Peter would show up when I was having a bad day? Instead he'd go hang out with his friends because he thought I was being a bummer.

My heart yearned for something I was afraid was impossible. Connor couldn't really be mine. We were just in each other's lives for a season and someday—probably soon—that season would be over and I'd be left feeling adrift and alone once again.

I shouldn't let him stay. I should take that bag of takeout —because let's be real, I wasn't about to pass up a chance for my favorite Chinese food—tell him it had been fun but we should end this, and let him be on his way.

I didn't do any of that.

Instead, I got on my tiptoes and kissed him. It wasn't a passionate kiss, or a quick peck on the lips. It was a kiss filled with tenderness, longing, and gratitude. Because after this spectacularly crummy day, just being near him was enough to make me feel better.

He set the food down on the small table where I'd left my keys and wrapped me in his arms as we kissed soft and slow. When I finally broke the kiss, he wouldn't let me pull any farther away.

"What was that for?"

"I'm just glad you're here." It was the truth, but only the tip of a very large iceberg of why I kissed him.

"Me too." And then his lips were back on mine, still soft and slow. The kiss was almost drugging in the way it made me feel light and airy.

His mouth moved down, nipping at that space between my neck and shoulder that always seemed to be a direct line to my clit. I squealed when he lifted me up without warning, carrying me down the hall to my bedroom.

He set me down by the edge of the bed and stared down at me with a glimmer in his eyes. Without breaking eye contact, I lifted my arms up straight. That stupid sexy smirk appeared on his face as he pulled my shirt up and over my head, dropping it on the floor. His pupils dilated as he wrapped his hand around my back and unclasped my bra. His gaze finally broke from mine, falling to my breasts. They were on the smaller side, but fit my frame well. My dusty-rose colored nipples were erect and eager for attention.

Connor's tongue licked across his bottom lip, mesmerizing me to distraction until he dipped his head and took one of my tight buds into his mouth. He sucked hard, and I inhaled a sharp breath as my hands automatically went to his head.

Holy shit.

"Do that again," I croaked.

He kept his mouth on my breast, even as he tipped his head so he could look up at me from his awkwardly hunched position. He sucked again, watching my face the entire time, and my legs shook from the pleasure that coursed through me from the pull on my nipple.

I whimpered when he pulled away, but any further complaints died in my throat when he laid me out on the bed so I could relax while he played with my breasts.

He cupped his large hand around one breast while his mouth covered the other one. He nipped at it with his teeth, and the spike of pleasure made me thrust my hips in the air.

"Hmm," he hummed against my breasts. "I should've played with these sooner. I didn't realize you were so sensitive."

"Neither did I," I mumbled, my brain fuzzy with lust. There was a lot Connor had taught me about my body in the short time we'd been together.

He pulled off with a pop and then his fierce gaze locked on mine. "You've never played with them yourself?"

I shook my head.

I don't know why. I'd masturbated, but playing with my breasts hadn't really been in the front of my mind. My focus had always been a quick release. It was almost mechanical, and the way he was looking at me now made me wonder if that wasn't normal.

Was this going to be another thing I'd done wrong? I couldn't bear the thought that it was another thing I'd failed at—not today.

"Jenna," he said, his voice ragged, and my name hung in the air like there was so much more he wanted to say. But instead of speaking again, he dropped his mouth back to my breasts, and between pinching, sucking, and fondling, he brought me to the edge of my peak and threw me right over it. I arched my back, crying out as the pleasure surged through me.

I sagged back against the bed, spent and blissed out.

"Holy shit. I didn't even know it was possible to come from breast stimulation."

He didn't say anything, so I looked over to find him pulling off his clothes while his hungry gaze ate me up. He didn't talk dirty like normal. Instead he put on a condom, spread out my legs, and slid right inside. I was soaked, so it was an easy glide, but he was big enough it was still a stretch.

I moaned and then wrapped my hands around his neck, pulling his chest down to mine. I needed to feel him over me, inside me, everywhere. I never wanted this to stop.

I didn't want to lose him.

And that scared the shit out of me.

"Connor," I whispered against his lips.

His eyes flared. "I know, Sugar. I've got you."

He did have me, more than he knew, and much more than I'd ever planned.

I was never going to survive the end of this.

He stared at me as he thrust home over and over until we were both sweaty, panting, and right on the edge of pure bliss. I dug my fingers into his ass, my legs wrapped around him as I tried to urge him on. I was so close, but he refused to go faster, to fuck me hard and rough like he'd always done. Instead, he kept the pace slow and steady and torturous.

I'd never considered sex lovemaking. Honestly, the phrase seemed cliché to me, but as he moved deeper into me and stared down at me like I held the moon and stars in my eyes, I couldn't help but feel like that's exactly what we were doing—making love.

The thought hit me right as my orgasm crashed into me and I exploded around him, my pussy clenching so hard, he grunted and then I felt his body tense as he let out his own groan, coming in the condom.

Not once did he break eye contact. Not until he collapsed to the side of me and held me close, my leg draped over his, my arm over his stomach while he held my back and his other hand rested on my hip. We lay there in silence for a while until sleep finally claimed me.

I woke with a start, disoriented in the dark. When had we turned off the lights? The sound that woke me up came again, and I turned to Connor who cried out in his sleep. The ambient glow of the streetlamps through my window gave enough light for me to see him. His chest was covered in sweat and his head thrashed side to side.

"No," he murmured, his voice broken and hoarse as if he had been screaming it for hours.

Tears filled my eyes as I tried to process how best to wake him up. I thought I remembered you weren't supposed to wake someone out of a nightmare because they might react poorly, but I couldn't bear to watch him suffer any longer.

I placed my hand on his sweaty chest. "Connor."

His legs thrashed against the loose sheet covering them and I pulled it off his body before trying again. "Connor. You need to wake up." I brushed my fingers over his short hair. "I'm right here. You're okay. Wake up."

His arm shot up and gripped my wrist, holding my hand to his chest at the same time that his eyes popped open, but it was like he was somewhere else, seeing something else. Then he blinked and sucked in a sharp breath before looking over at me. "Jenna?"

"I'm here," I said, curling up against him. He pulled me into his arms, holding me tight like he was afraid I might let him go.

We didn't speak for a while, but I couldn't go back to sleep. My heart ached for him, and I wanted to ease some of his burden the way he always eased mine.

I waited until I felt his heart return to its normal steady rhythm from where I rested my head on his chest.

"Do you want to talk about it?"

He didn't reply, but he tensed, and we were so close together there was no way I could miss it.

"Did something happen when you were in the army?" I asked, trying to keep my voice soft so he'd know this was a safe space to share. I'd heard stories of soldiers returning home with PTSD, but Connor had never shared anything about his time in the military with me. He still kept his past close to the vest.

But after the way he'd made love to me earlier, I didn't want him to keep those parts of himself from me anymore.

He inhaled deeply and let it out slowly. For a second, I thought he would finally talk to me, but then he flipped us over so he was between my legs. There was a smile on his mouth, but it didn't meet his eyes.

"I can think of something else I'd rather do."

My heart dropped as he started kissing his way down my still naked body.

I put my hands on his neck trying to stop his movements. "Connor."

He pushed up on his arms so he caged me. "No, I don't want to talk about it, Jenna. I want to fuck you." He smiled again, probably hoping it would take the sting out of his words. "If you're willing to help me clear my head, then spread those legs, darlin'."

My legs were already spread since he was currently between them, but I understood what he was doing—getting my permission to deflect using sex.

Emotion clogged my throat as it became clear he didn't want to let me in. He wanted to keep the status quo. I don't know what earlier was about, but I wished he'd never made love to me because now I knew the difference. And whatever this was, it was a poor substitute for what I really wanted.

I wanted him to be vulnerable with me the way I was vulnerable with him.

But now I needed out of my head too, so I spread my legs farther and pulled his mouth to mine. If he wanted to use sex to escape, then so would I.

He broke our kiss and moved down my body, spreading my legs and plundering my pussy with that ridiculously skilled mouth of his. My heart ached even as my body rose to attention, desperate for more pleasure.

He brought me over the cliff two more times—once with his mouth and another with his cock—until I was too exhausted to think.

I fell asleep wrapped in his arms, my body spent from pleasure but my heart feeling like it'd just gone through a cheese grater.

When was I going to learn not to let my heart get involved?

Rule #13

THE LESS SAID, THE BETTER

CONNOR

My phone buzzed in my pocket, and like a fucking addict, I ripped it out in record time, a smile spreading across my face as I opened Jenna's text. She was asleep when I snuck out this morning, too spent from last night.

Something I'd done on purpose.

It was getting harder and harder to battle the conflict raging inside me. A part of me wanted to tell her so desperately, to cut myself open and spill my guts to her because I knew only she could soothe the ever-present ache I'd carried since the ambush. But the other part of me knew she didn't deserve to carry that burden. Those were my ghosts to battle, not hers.

I'd been holding her at bay, but the nightmare was unexpected. I'd had them for months after the ambush and before my service commitment was up, but I hadn't had a single one since I'd started staying the night with Jenna.

Why it had to happen last night of all nights was a real

kick to the nuts. I'd made love to Jenna and fallen asleep with her in my arms, more content than I'd felt in my whole life. Then I'd woken up in a panic—chest heaving and covered in sweat—with a concerned Jenna staring down at me. I hadn't expected it, but maybe I should have.

Regardless, I know I didn't handle it right. She wanted to talk, to understand, but I couldn't dump all of that on her.

I don't think I could've forced the words out if I even tried. Most days I felt trapped in my own body when it came to talking about that day, and the army had been such an integral part of my life for so long that it felt impossible to talk about *anything* without coming back to it.

Which meant Jenna was getting a lot less from me than she deserved.

I knew it, but didn't know how to fix it. Not yet at least.

The only thing I could think to do was fuck her so hard she was too tired to talk, but even as I watched her come—twice—I couldn't ignore the tinge of hurt in her otherwise beautiful gaze.

Leaving while she was still asleep was my second bad decision in less than twenty-four hours, but there was nothing I could do about it. She was dead to the world and I had to get to work before Wyatt skinned me alive.

Ever since that barbecue, he'd gone from a chill and insightful supervisor to an extreme hard-ass who threatened to write me up if I breathed wrong.

"What did I say about personal texts during work?"

Speak of the devil.

I glanced up from my phone to find him staring me down, his mouth in a hard line and his eyes glaring. "Who are you texting that has you grinning like an idiot?"

His words seemed playful which was so incongruous with the look on his face. I didn't answer him as I slid my phone in my pocket, which only made his glare even more glacial.

"We have a red carpet event tomorrow night. You think you can follow the protocol for a few hours?"

I wanted to ask him what crawled up his ass, but I already knew. He was on to me. And he wasn't buying any of the bullshit I'd been slinging claiming that Jenna and I were just talking because of that stupid reception.

"Yes, sir."

I'd learned sometimes it was better to say as little as possible, but Wyatt was ex-military too. His jaw clenched and he took a step closer. "I swear to God if you hurt her, I'll skin you alive. Got it?"

He stared at me, his hard glare zeroing on my eyes, and that's when I saw it—the worry. He wasn't just being a hard-ass to be a hard-ass. He was worried about her—what I'd do to her—and after the way I'd mangled things last night, maybe he was right to be worried.

The tension in my shoulders dropped and my voice was genuine when I said, "Yes, sir." Because I had no intention of hurting Jenna. I'd been in this from the very beginning. I may not be ready to spill my guts out to her yet, but I'd never purposefully hurt her.

"You're free to go," he said, seeming reluctant, but I didn't stick around long enough for him to change his mind.

I pulled up to Jenna's house more nervous than I'd ever been. I'd never hurt a woman I was falling in love with, so I wasn't really sure how to handle the situation. I had a bouquet of her favorite flowers—dahlias—and a bag of her favorite candy—ROLO caramels—but I wasn't sure it would be enough to get her to forget about last night and put us back where we were before my nightmare fucked it all up.

I knocked on her door and waited patiently for her to

open it. There was a shuffling and then she opened the door wearing my favorite outfit—a loose sweater and leggings. I didn't know why it was my favorite, except that I loved how relaxed she looked whenever she wore it.

Except she didn't look as relaxed as normal. She looked guarded, and I couldn't ignore the fact that she didn't smile at me like she normally did when I came over. My stomach twisted painfully and my chest felt tight.

"Hey," I said.

"Hi." She leaned against the doorframe, her gaze dropping to the flowers and chocolate in my hands.

"I know this doesn't make up for last night, but I'm hoping it's a start."

She stared at me wordlessly, her eyes darting back and forth between mine and her teeth nibbling on her lower lip.

"I'm sorry," I said.

It was all I *could* say until I could figure out how to get the words out without my body physically going on lockdown. But I had a sinking feeling in my gut that it wasn't enough, and I was running out of time if I didn't figure my shit out soon.

She released her lip and stepped back, allowing me room to walk in, but her beautiful smile was still missing. She walked over to her couch, pulling a blanket over her and then grabbing the remote. I set the stuff I'd brought for her down on her coffee table and then sat beside her.

"I hope you like rom-coms because I'm not changing my movie for you."

I fought my smile. I'd never seen this side of her before, and even though I hated being the cause of her upset, I couldn't deny she was kind of cute when she was sulking.

"Rom-coms are fine with me." Honestly, I'd watch

anything she wanted as long as it meant she wasn't kicking me out.

Because it meant she hadn't given up on me yet.

Rule #14

WHEN YOU OPEN UP, OTHERS WILL OPEN UP TOO

JENNA

I'd always thought that phrase "like a chicken with your head cut off" was weird. Maybe because I'd never been around farm animals or seen a chicken with its head cut off, but I suddenly had a greater appreciation for it. Nothing else came close to comparing how I felt as we neared the reception for my mom and her new husband. It was two days away, and the number of things I still had to do to pull it off in a way that wouldn't get me a guilt trip from my mom made my head spin.

My apartment was covered in tulle and packages of Jordan almonds. My mom's reception wish list had been clear that she wanted these at every place setting. Considering I wasn't going to be able to get the monogrammed placemats because of a backorder issue, this was something I was determined to finish.

A key jingled in the lock and then Connor was opening the door, his arms full of groceries because I was completely out of food and he'd insisted on stopping by the store on his way home.

Not that he lived here. He didn't. Just because he was here every night and hadn't been back to Grant's in a week and had a key didn't mean he was living here.

It was just easier.

I scrubbed my forehead with the tips of my fingers. My denial game had gotten really good since we'd gotten together. Hell, maybe it had always been this good. Maybe that was why I'd never seen the signs of Sadie and my dad hooking up behind my back.

No, I couldn't think about that right now. I was happy for them and didn't have brain space to spare feeling anything besides focused on wrapping these fucking Jordan almonds.

What genius came up with this idea anyway? Did they actually do this themselves or were they rich enough to realize that it's a real giant pain in the ass to individually wrap Jordan almonds in tulle.

Connor looked around the room, his frown hard to miss, but I decided to ignore it and kept on tying the ribbon around this particular bundle.

"I'm really starting to hate your mom," he grumbled. "This is ridiculous, Jenna."

I dropped my hands in my lap as my shoulders fell in defeat and tears threatened to fall. "This is literally the only thing from her binder that I can make happen in our time-frame. Can you just help me?"

It was hard to ignore the look of pity on his face when I was staring right at it, so I looked away. I finished tying the bow and set this bundle aside. Only another hundred to go.

I'd already done three hundred, but our parents had a

guest list two hundred people long, and my mom was insistent that each person should get one at their seat and then another for when they leave. I doubted they'd even eat them all and we'd probably have hundreds left over, but that didn't stop me from continuing to make bundle after bundle.

Large hands covered mine, stopping my movement. I looked up to find Connor only inches away, his brow furrowed in what could only be described as concern. His other hand brushed a loose hair from my face.

"I hate seeing you beat yourself up for her when she doesn't appreciate it or deserve it. You're too good for her, Jenna."

The sincerity in his voice was my tipping point, and just like that, the dam broke. My shoulders shook as tears fell and before I even had a chance to ask, his arms were wrapped around me and he was hauling me into his lap, holding me tight. His lips pressed against my head in a tender kiss that had my heart hurting for a different reason. I sobbed in his arms, years of built-up feelings that I'd tried to shove down bursting forth uncontrollably. I had some sense that this was a ridiculously over-the-top response to what he'd said, but I guess there was only so much a person could push down before it all came bubbling up to the surface with no chance of stopping until everything was out.

We sat there for minutes, me sobbing into his chest while he held me tight and whispered softly into my hair. I was too distraught and caught up in my own emotions to make out any of the words, but just knowing he was here, that he had me, was enough to ease the worst of the heartache.

The sobs turned into hiccups, and then just sniffles. Snot was running out of my nose and I'd never felt less attractive than I did right then. I was afraid to look up at him, but I knew I'd have to face him at some point. He was too attuned to me. He'd realize I was ready to talk and he'd make me.

If only I had the same ability to make him spill all his secrets to me.

He tucked his finger under my chin and lifted my face so he could stare into my tear-stained eyes. "You ready to talk about it?"

I looked into his dark eyes wondering what it would take for him to finally let me in—all the way in—the way I was letting him in with every moment we spent together. Maybe if I told him everything, he'd do the same. Telling him my favorite things and the bits about Peter and my mom that I'd shared weren't the same as opening up all my hurts and insecurities.

"My mom and I have always had a complicated relationship. I was never girly enough for her—"

"You mean vapid," he interrupted.

I stared at him, wondering how he could deduce that so quickly. His eyes softened. "Jenna, you're plenty girly. You love pink and purple and pop music and probably pumpkin spice lattes."

I did love pumpkin spice lattes. And all those other things were true too.

"So girly isn't your problem. You're not shallow like your mom, and any Joe off the street would be able to figure that out after only about five minutes. Or less."

"Okay, fine, girly isn't the right word. Maybe it's that I'm not as vapid, as you said, but regardless, there's always been a tension between us that I never saw between other girls and their moms. Sadie was never close to her mom, which is maybe why we clung to each other like we did. We'd been missing something, and we both accepted the other exactly as we were. My mom only made time for me when it was useful for her. My parents divorced when I was four, and even though initially they were supposed to have joint custody and split their time with me equally, my mom decided she wanted the flexibility to travel and be out late without me ruining her fun. So I ended up living with my dad full-time. My dad did his best and he's great, but I've always hoped that if I just did *more* that maybe my mom would finally tell me she loved me and actually mean it. That sounds stupid because there are kids with no parents, but it's how I felt—feel."

"It's not stupid."

I took a deep breath. This next part was harder to confess. "She was proud of me when I got into vet school. She told everyone about it—how smart I was and that I was going to be a pet doctor. For the first time, I felt like I was good enough. She wasn't just proud of me, she was proud of me for pursuing something that I loved and was excited about."

I looked down at my hands in my lap. "But I'm not doing well at school. I'm way behind all my classmates, and this past semester, I almost failed. As it stands, I got a D in one of my core classes which means I need to retake it because I have to get a C or higher for it to count toward my degree. I wasn't originally planning to come home this summer. I was going to get an internship near school and try to make up the class over the summer so I could still graduate on time, but my advisor told me she thought that what I needed to do was reevaluate if this was the right career path for me."

I'd never felt as low as I did sitting in Dr. Washington's office listening to her crush all my dreams with every word out of her mouth. She thought I could *maybe* be a decent vet tech, but I didn't want to be a vet tech. There was nothing wrong with that job except that it wasn't the job for me. I wanted to be a veterinarian. I cried the whole way back to my apartment after that meeting. I'd never had someone tell me outright that they didn't think I should pursue my dreams.

"She basically told me to my face I wasn't good enough. It kind of sent me into a spiral," I admitted. "Instead of finding an internship, I called my friend who I knew was looking for someone to sublease down here and made arrangements for this apartment over the summer. At the end of the term, while all my peers started their internships, I was driving back home to figure out if I could really hack it in vet school, or if I should even try."

"And what have you decided?" he asked, his voice low and soothing.

"What do you mean?"

"Well, you've been here for a month already, right? So what have you decided to do?"

I shrugged against him. "I'm still not sure."

Quiet fell between us, and the gentle steadiness of his breathing against me lulled me into a peaceful state. The silence felt nice instead of scary or suffocating.

"You're good enough, Jenna."

He didn't whisper it or hesitate. The words came out clear and strong like he was announcing an irrefutable fact. I wished I could be as certain as he seemed to be.

"Tell me something about you," I said, my voice softer than I'd like.

His body stiffened so subtly that I wouldn't have noticed if I wasn't plastered against him. "What do you want to know?" he asked, but there was an undercurrent of dread in his voice.

"Anything." But there was something I was especially curious about, especially after his nightmare. "Why'd you leave the army?"

There was a pause—a moment where the air almost seemed charged with something—and then he was moving, shoving aside all the tulle and Jordan almond packages and then laying me down on the carpeted floor.

His eyes lit up with heat and that smirk was back on his face, but I knew him now—knew him better than he probably wanted me to since he wouldn't *tell* me anything—and I could see he was deflecting before the words even left his mouth. "That's a boring story. I'd much rather fuck you so hard you can't see straight."

Either something truly awful had happened during his time in the army...or he just didn't want to tell me anything about himself because this didn't mean to him what I could no longer deny it meant to me.

I wasn't sure which option hurt my heart more, but I knew I couldn't have sex with him in my current mental state. My tears weren't just about my pending decision about school or my mom, but the uncertainty I felt with him after the other night. Despite my better judgment—despite *knowing* he was likely going to break my heart from the very beginning—I'd fallen for him. My stupid heart hadn't needed words or his life story. It loved the way he made me feel whole, cherished, appreciated. His actions had convinced my dumbass heart that we weren't going to be crushed. But I'd just laid myself out bare for him and he was deflecting with sex again instead of giving me what I needed from him.

I couldn't do it.

I put a hand on his chest, and because I loved him, I tried to cushion my rejection with a weak smile.

"Not tonight, okay. I really just want to finish this and go to bed. I'm exhausted." It wasn't a lie, but it also wasn't the truth. His smile faltered, but he nodded his head and sat back, helping me up. We spent the rest of the night tying Jordan almonds while the TV played a show in the background. We didn't talk, and when we crawled into bed, I knew we wouldn't have sex tonight or any other night in the future. I couldn't allow my heart to continue on this path. I couldn't get invested in a relationship with a man who always held me at arm's length. I knew my worth now because of Connor.

And I knew I deserved more than this.

I always knew this had an expiration date, but tonight had proved to me that if I wanted to save myself from a heartbreak like I'd never felt before, this *had* to end.

Sooner rather than later.

Rule #15

DON'T BE SURPRISED WHEN YOUR CHANCES RUN OUT

CONNOR

I always knew this reception was going to be a disaster. What I hadn't expected was the tension to come from Jenna and me just as much as it came from our parents.

Jenna had been even more distant since her meltdown over Jordan almonds and her confession about vet school a couple of nights ago.

I knew what was bothering her. I'd known the second she shut me down that night. It was the first time she'd turned down sex since we got together, and I knew I was riding a thin line of being able to salvage this relationship. But I needed her to give me a little more time. I knew what she wanted, and I was trying to work through my mental blocks to encourage the words to come, but nothing I tried helped. Not that I really knew what to try. I didn't exactly grow up in a family that was open about their feelings or failures. You kept that shit to yourself.

That philosophy had served me just fine my entire adult life until now.

Even knowing what was bothering her, I didn't know how or when I'd get a chance to fix it. It wasn't like I could pull her aside and dump my baggage on her while we were trying to handle the clusterfuck that was our parents. If I could even force the words out of my throat.

If I thought things were tense with me and Jenna, it was only a fraction of the glacial chill between our parents. They came in separate vehicles and hadn't spoken a single word to each other the entire time. My dad was over talking with his friends, and Jenna's mom was on the opposite side of the room talking to hers.

I was impressed by the turnout considering it was clear by the looks of the guests that everyone knew this reception was a total joke. There was no love apparent between my dad and Jenna's mom. My only question at this point was if they'd make it to the end of the reception before they announced they were getting divorced. Should they even open the gifts, or should I hand them back to the guests as they left?

These were all questions I would've asked Jenna and we'd probably laugh about how predictable our parents were, but Jenna was very clearly ignoring my existence.

I glanced over at her to gauge what the odds were of her letting me approach without finding an excuse to walk away when I caught the tail end of her mom's comment to her friends. "Jordan almonds are so last season. I wanted these fancy honey-dipped pistachios dusted with gold flakes that I'd seen in a magazine, but this was all Jenna could find. She's not as connected as we are, but that's okay, sweetheart. You tried." She patted Jenna on the shoulder before focusing solely on her friends while my gaze hyperfocused on the only woman in this building who mattered at all.

Her face was devoid of emotion, but I was observant

and I'd made it my purpose to know every nuance of Jenna's expressions. And no matter how well Jenna tried to hold herself together, her eyes would always give her away if you looked close enough.

The devastating heartbreak she was trying so hard to hide was what broke my resolve to keep my distance until we could talk privately.

Fuck that.

I was done appeasing her mom's bullshit. Not when she couldn't even give Jenna a thank you for all the time and tears she'd put into this Titanic-level disaster of a wedding reception.

I walked over with purpose, thankful the distance was so short, then gently grabbed Jenna above the elbow. I pasted on the fakest smile I could manage. "Excuse me, ladies. I need to steal Jenna away."

The only acknowledgment I got was a quick perusal from the ladies checking me out, but Jenna's mom didn't stop telling whatever stupid story she was spewing. What a fucking bitch.

I pulled Jenna back and then marched us through the guests until we were walking down the hall into an empty side room I'd noticed earlier. I guided her inside before I let her go and closed the door, leaning against it so she couldn't make up some bullshit excuse to escape.

She crossed her arms over her chest and stared at the floor. "What did you need?"

I hated how empty her voice sounded. Jenna was warmth and peace and happiness. This wasn't *my* Jenna, and I needed my Jenna back. I could feel the cold seeping into my veins, and I couldn't be strong for us both if I let that cold infiltrate any further.

I stepped closer but stopped when she took a step back.

I clenched my jaw and asked the question I already knew the answer to. "What's going on?"

She kept her head dipped, and I wondered if she was going to ignore the question, but then she looked up at me and there was so much fire and hurt in her gaze, it almost made me take a step back.

"What's going on? Well, let's see. My ungrateful mother has done nothing but complain the entire night about every-thing I *didn't* do instead of acknowledging all the work I did for her stupid reception. To top that off, your dad is being a giant dick to anyone who isn't his friend."

I had missed that last one, so I made a mental note to pull my dad aside and get him in line. But I knew that was only the tip of the iceberg.

"And us?" I prompted.

Her arms dropped to her sides and her shoulders slouched as her gaze traced my face like this was the last time she was going to see me and she wanted to remember it. I knew that look.

"There is no us, Connor."

The cold I'd been holding back swept over me so swiftly it was hard to breathe.

No, no, no. She couldn't be doing this now. I needed more time.

"We should've never hooked up, but whatever it was, it's over now. I don't want to see you after this reception," she said, her tone final.

No.

The word was right there on the tip of my tongue, but I couldn't get it out of my mouth. My body was frozen, my heart clenching so painfully tight it felt like she was ripping it out of me.

She swiped a tear from her eye and then she was

moving, darting past my body where I'd left a gap behind me and sneaking out the door.

No. This wasn't how we ended. We weren't supposed to end at all. She could be mad at me and tell me I needed to tell her everything about my past, but she wasn't supposed to just give up and walk away. How could she just walk away? Didn't she feel the connection between us? It was deeper than anything I'd ever felt and it wasn't just sex.

It was the quiet moments when we held each other before sleep took us. It was making dinner together and laughing or dancing in the kitchen while we waited for it to finish cooking. It was playing card games in our underwear. It was me holding her while she cried and opened up to me.

I knew I'd made a mistake not telling her about my leaving the army when she asked. But I'd had no idea it had been a fatal error. And fatal was the only way to describe it because standing here without her and knowing she was certain it needed to be over felt like dying.

I walked back out to the reception on autopilot, but my gaze was focused on one person only—Jenna. I tucked my hand in my pocket and felt the thick cardstock between my fingers. I needed time to regroup—to figure out how the hell to fix this, because there had to be a way.

I couldn't lose her. But I knew better than to push it today—here—when she was already feeling weak and hurt by her mom.

So instead, I found her by the caterer and pulled out the card and handed it to her. She looked at me before looking down at the business card.

With her brow furrowed, she asked, "What's this?"

"It's the name of a vet I reached out to. He's looking for an intern for the rest of the summer and said you sounded perfect. All you have to do is call him to set it up."

She stared down at the card and then up at me, her gorgeous hazel eyes filled with confusion, hurt, and something that could only be described as longing.

I needed to leave, or I was going to get on my knees right here and beg her not to give up on me. That I could try to open up and tell her everything I'd kept buried deep down.

But there was one more thing I had to say to her before I left. One more truth I needed her to believe. I stepped into her space and dipped my head until my mouth was right by her ear. "You are good enough. Always. Please don't ever doubt that." My voice cracked at the end, and I knew I was perilously close to breaking in front of her.

I spun around and walked away from the only woman I'd ever loved, leaving my heart in her hands.

Rule #16

DON'T ROCK THE BOAT

JENNA

"Jenna, did you hear me?"

My mom's voice broke through my brain fog. It had been two days since their disaster of a reception and my breakup with Connor, and in those two days, I'd done nothing.

I came home, sat down on my couch, and cried. Once the tears subsided, I didn't have any energy to move, so I stayed there. I probably would have still been there if my mom hadn't called me this morning and demanded that I join her for brunch.

You'd think I'd be ravenous after subsisting on crackers and Pop-Tarts for the last two days, but my stomach was in knots.

Everything felt *wrong*.

"Jenna!"

Mom shouted my name and then glanced around, offering an apologetic smile to the few people that were around us.

"Sorry, what were you saying?"

She huffed and then took a sip of her mimosa before facing me with a somber expression. "Dick and I have decided to get divorced."

Color me shocked.

I stared at her, waiting for more, but she arched a brow at me like she was expecting me to say something.

"Shocker."

My eyes widened at the same time hers did and I slapped my hand over my mouth. I couldn't believe I'd just said that. Sure, I was thinking it, but I've thought plenty of things about my mom's relationships over the years and never once have I slipped up in front of her.

"Jenna Marie Jones, I did not raise you to speak to me that way. The least you can do is show some compassion. Can't you tell I'm devastated?"

Nope. I couldn't. There wasn't even a glistening in her eyes to suggest she was working up some tears. Her tone was completely unaffected, and her expression told me she was more upset I didn't bend over backward to console her than the fact that her latest marriage was over.

And then it hit me. Why was I always protecting her feelings? Why didn't I tell her the truth?

It would likely blow up in my face, but what exactly did I have to lose? So I let loose.

"You don't look devastated at all. And why should you be? You knew him, what, for all of a month?"

"Jenna!"

"No. You don't get to act all butt hurt because I'm not fawning all over you. I'm going through my own shit and you never, ever ask me about my feelings or give a shit how I'm doing. So why should I care about your feelings? You go through men like people go through disposable water bottles. I don't even remember most of their names or attempt to learn anything about them because I know it won't matter. The only person you love is yourself, and I'm sick of pretending that our relationship will ever be more than...this," I finished, gesturing between us with a limp hand.

Mom stared at me like she didn't recognize me—like some alien had taken over her daughter.

Right about now was when the shame and guilt should start to eat at me, but it didn't come. Instead, I felt lighter. I felt free. I didn't have to keep up this stupid charade. I didn't have to attempt to appease her when I knew nothing I did would ever be enough for her. But not because of me, because of *her*. She wasn't enough for herself, so how could anyone else possibly be?

I pushed away from the table. "It's been a rough few days for me, and I don't want to be here anymore, so I'm going home. Thanks for brunch."

I stood and looked at my mom, who was gaping at me like a fish out of water, then turned and walked away. It wasn't until I was home that the feelings I'd pushed away to be functional in public hit me hard.

My apartment felt empty without him here.

I felt empty.

The tears I thought I'd cried out two days ago came back with a vengeance, and I sagged against the door and then slid down until my butt hit the floor. The last time I was in this position, Connor knocked on the door and made it all better. Another flood of tears let loose as I sobbed into my arms wishing he was here this time, but I couldn't keep sacrificing myself for other people.

I couldn't hand him my heart if he couldn't even tell me anything significant about his life.

My phone dinged, and my stupid heart fluttered with hope thinking it might be Connor only to crash down into my stomach when it wasn't him, but Sadie.

I'm in the neighborhood. Can I swing by?

If she came over now there'd be no way to hide that I'd been crying. She'd want to know what was wrong, and more than anything, I wanted to lean on her the way I always used to before she got together with my dad.

I wanted my best friend.

Sure.

She showed up five minutes later, and the second I opened the door, concern filled her blue eyes. "What's wrong?"

Whatever semblance of "put together" I had crumbled at her question. Not even two seconds and she knew. My mom spent at least half an hour with me before my outburst and never once asked if I was okay.

Sadie didn't need an invite. She stepped inside and pulled me into her arms, hugging me hard and taking all my weight as my body sagged against her. "I've got you," she murmured as she walked us toward the couch and we sat down. "Did something happen with Connor?"

She said it like she already knew the answer, and I remembered how destroyed she was when my dad ended things between them out of some misplaced loyalty to me. I cared more that he'd lied than that he fell in love with her.

Sadie was amazing. I'd think he was a bigger idiot if he hadn't fallen for her.

I pulled away and grabbed a tissue off the coffee table, blowing my nose and then sagging back against the couch.

"I ended it."

"Why? I thought everything was going so well."

I was already shaking my head before she finished. "He won't open up to me."

She furrowed her brow. "What do you mean?"

I sat up, and for the second time in a week, I poured out my soul and shared with her everything I'd been keeping to myself until I spilled it all with Connor. I told her all about vet school, Connor's use of sex to avoid talking about himself, what happened at the reception, and then finished by telling her about my disastrous brunch with my mom this morning.

"I can't believe you've been carrying all this by yourself." Her own insecurities flickered in her eyes. "You used to tell me this stuff when it was happening, not months later."

"I know. It's just different now."

"Jenna, if you don't want your dad to know, you can tell me and I'll keep it a secret until you're ready to tell him. I never want you to feel like you can't trust me just because he and I are together."

"It's not that. Not really, anyway. It's that you have someone. You tell him everything first." She opened her mouth, but I held up a hand to stop her. "And that's how it should be. I'm just feeling a little lost. I don't have a person, and my life feels like a mess of epic proportions right now. Me not telling you was never really about you, it's about me and getting in my own head about stuff."

She didn't look like she believed me. "You're sure?"

I grabbed her hand and squeezed it once. "I'm sure. I'm sorry I haven't talked to you about any of this." I sagged against the couch, the weight of everything I'd been carrying hitting me. "Everyone's got their life together and I'm floundering. I feel like someone threw me in a pool and I can't figure out which way is up."

"First of all, it may appear that everyone's got their life together, but that's rarely the truth. There's always some aspect that they're neglecting, so you're not the only one who struggles. Second," she started, dipping her head down to make sure I was looking at her, "about the whole vet school thing—"

"I know. I need to figure it out before I have to pay next semester's tuition, especially if I'm not going to go back."

"Jenna, do you want to be a vet?"

My heart clenched as she watched me with complete openness. "Yes," I mumbled, then cleared my throat and said louder, "Yes."

She smiled. "Then don't let those pretentious fuckers tell you that you can't. You go back to that school and prove to them how amazing you are. The summer's not over. Do you think there's a chance you could find a vet down here to intern with until you go back? Maybe it'd be good to get some perspective and work with someone who's not in that program or tied to it."

The card that Connor handed me before he walked out of the reception flashed in my mind.

"Actually, there is someone."

"Well, then what are you waiting for? Call them now! Or we could drive to the office."

Her excitement was contagious and soon we were both smiling. Sadie stayed on my couch while I called, and I didn't miss the way her brow arched when I explained that Connor had reached out and suggested I call. The nurse on the line knew exactly who I was talking about, and before I knew it I had an appointment for tomorrow to meet with Dr. Cunningham.

Sadie stayed late, and we spent most of the night gorging on pizza, catching up, and talking about everything and nothing. It was the exact kind of night I didn't realize I needed.

But when she left, I couldn't deny that the void Connor's absence had left was still noticeable. Maybe less so when Sadie was around, but in the short time we'd been together, he'd managed to embed himself into my very being—or at least that's what it felt like.

As I tossed and turned, I wondered if he'd ever be able to open up to someone, and tried to ignore the pain of knowing I'd never get that piece of him, no matter how badly I wanted it.

Rule #17

FRIENDS SUPPORT YOU EVEN WHEN THEY THINK YOU'RE STUPID

CONNOR

This show was dumb, but the remote was too far away to bother changing it to something else. Why did Grant even have cable? Didn't he know people our age only used streaming services anymore? The door opened and Grant walked in, letting out a heavy sigh before he dropped his keys on the little bowl he had on the kitchen counter. His wallet was next.

"Hey, will you grab me a beer?" I hollered at him from the couch.

"No."

I glanced up at him, sure I heard him wrong, but his glare kept my snarky reply from escaping my mouth.

He took a step closer to the couch. "What the fuck are you doing, man?"

I pointed to the TV. "I know this show is stupid, but I've only been watching it for like twenty minutes."

"I'm not talking about the TV show"—he glanced over

and grimaced—"which I one hundred percent agree is stupid. I'm talking about Jenna."

I looked away, focusing on the screen as if this show was the most interesting thing I'd ever watched while I tried to ignore the way my heart felt like it was being poked with a seven-inch needle. "Oh."

He moved until he was in front of me, blocking my view of the TV. "Oh? That's seriously all you have to say? Why aren't you fighting for her? Sadie came into work and practically ripped me a new asshole telling me what a spectacularly shitty friend I had, and I couldn't even argue with her because I have no fucking clue why you're sitting on my couch and letting the best thing you ever had slip right through your goddamn fingers."

I shoved off the couch and headed toward the guest room. I didn't need to hear this from him—I was beating myself up enough as it was.

"Connor," he called to my back, but I just kept walking, my pulse spiking and my stomach tightening.

There was an energy swirling in my gut—one I always got when I was about to blow—and Grant didn't deserve to be on the other end of my self-loathing.

But he just wouldn't quit.

"Connor! Jenna may have let you walk away for being a fucking dumbass, but I've been your best friend for as long as I can remember, and I'm not about to let you fuck this up any more than you already have. Turn around and fucking talk."

That was it. I spun around and got in his face. "You think I don't want to? You think I want to hold all this shit in and let it fester and destroy the best relationship of my entire life? Fuck you."

"Talk to me," he said, concern filling his blue eyes.

"I fucking *can't*," I gritted. If I could, I wouldn't be in this mess to begin with.

"Yes, you can. You open your mouth and words come out. You're doing it right now. Don't be a jackass. Tell me what's going on."

I scrubbed my hand over my hair and then, like air being let out of a balloon, all my anger and self-hatred whooshed out of me and I was left feeling empty and weak.

"The words won't come." I was embarrassed by the way my voice cracked. It was the first time in my entire life I'd been embarrassed in front of Grant. I'd always been strong and sure, sometimes goofy, but never weak—not like this.

But I was weak now, and I could barely hold myself up from the weight of that weakness bearing down on me.

Understanding dawned on his face. "You *can't* talk." He finally got it. "What the hell happened to you over there?" he asked, his voice low and worried.

I shot him a look, and he dropped his head back with another heavy sigh. "Right. Sorry." He fixed his gaze back on me. "You want to tell her, don't you?"

"If you think for a second I wanted *this* outcome, you're the idiot, not me."

"Do you love her?"

Yes. But I wouldn't tell it to him until I'd told her.

If I ever got the chance.

If I could just unlock the damn metaphorical box that held all my words hostage—the most important ones at least, the ones Jenna wanted—then maybe I'd finally get the chance to tell her the three words that would be true whether she heard them or not.

For the rest of my life, I'd love her.

My phone beeped in my pocket, and I pulled it out without hesitation, always hoping it would be her, but instead it was someone I hadn't spoken to in months. I read his text, wondering if there was maybe someone else who understood the choke hold I was experiencing.

"I gotta go," I told Grant.

"Was that her?"

"No, but maybe it's someone who can help me find a way to get her back."

Without a backward glance, I was out the door.

I was the first one to the bar, so I grabbed a stool at the counter and ordered a beer. My fingernail scraped against the moisture on the beer bottle, my gaze staring vacantly at the woodgrain of the bar top. This last week had been hell. If I thought I was wrecked after what happened overseas, it was nothing compared to the hollowness of losing Jenna.

It was made worse knowing I could've prevented it if I could've just opened my fucking mouth.

Why was it so hard to tell her what happened? To tell her *anything* about my life. Maybe because I hadn't told anyone anything personal since the army. Hell, even then, I'd barely scraped the surface about my personal life. Only my closest friends knew about the strained relationship I had with my parents.

But Jenna still deserved better. She opened up to me when she didn't have to. She let herself be vulnerable, so why the fuck couldn't I?

I brought the bottle up to my lips and took a long sip, wishing it could wash away the guilt and loss and ache of missing her.

A hand slapped my back, and I looked behind me, but he'd already moved to my other side. "How's it going, Cowboy?" Ryan Hurley asked as he sat down on the stool next to me. My gaze dropped to the prosthetic limb where his right leg used to be, and that guilt in my stomach swirled violently. His gaze followed mine, but he didn't seem nearly as affected as I was.

Hurley and I were in the same unit in the army. Only three of us made it out of that hellhole, and I'm not sure I'll ever forgive myself for the role I played in putting us in that situation.

Hurley watched me with an almost clinical gaze before he stated, "You still haven't talked to that therapist I recommended."

He'd suggested one right after I got discharged, but I'd thrown that card in a pile and never looked at it again. I didn't even know what happened to it.

"No," I said, my voice low and weak.

He frowned and then lifted a hand for the bartender's attention. "I'll have what he's having," he said, and the bartender quickly flipped the top off and handed him the icy bottle of beer. He took a hearty sip, staring straight forward before he spun and faced me.

"Did I ever tell you why I started seeing that therapist?"

"I assumed because it was recommended. You always were a rule follower." Hurley was the Boy Scout and good boy of our group, but all that preparedness was for nothing when the ambush hit.

I took another hearty sip of my beer, trying to wash away the never-ending guilt.

"I was going to kill myself."

I snapped my head to face him and saw the truth in his gaze, but he nodded to confirm it was true. "My wife caught me." He did look away then, but I'd recognized the shame in his eyes before he'd turned away. "I'll never forgive myself for what I put her through, or that she saw me like that, but she saved my life. And then she forced me to go to therapy. She found the therapist, and I only went that first time because she drove me. I expected to find some woman there trying to get me to share my feelings, but instead it was an army vet who'd also lost his leg. I'm not really sure how he did it because that first meeting is a bit of a blur, but he got me to talk, and I've been going every week ever since. He's a good guy, knows his shit, and if you can't talk to me or Cody, you should talk to him."

Cody Maxwell was the only other survivor from our unit, and even though he'd reached out a few times, I'd been too chickenshit to call him back. Hurley only got me out tonight because I was sick of staring at Grant's TV.

"I...I can't talk to anybody." If I couldn't talk to Jenna, I doubted anyone could get me to share. She'd been the first person to make me feel anything besides guilt since I returned stateside.

Hurley rested his hand on my shoulder. "I know the feeling, brother, and it took rock fucking bottom for me to open up, but I wouldn't go back now. It's scary as shit at first, but eventually it feels fucking good to let it all out. If you keep it bottled up, you're going to ruin your life. Trust me."

I already felt like I had. I'd lost Jenna.

So what else did I have to lose at this point?

Rule #18

BARING YOUR SOUL IS EASY

CONNOR

I sat down on the small sofa in Dr. Hoffman's spacious office. He sat in a chair opposite me and rested his chin in his hand. I pulled at the thighs of my jeans, then rubbed my hands along the seams on the sides, the friction grounding me as I waited for him to say or do something. Eventually his silent watching was too much.

"Aren't you supposed to ask me questions or some shit?"

He smiled, the right side of his mouth pulling up slightly. "Or some shit."

I blinked. What the hell did that mean? I looked at the door and then back at him. "I don't know how to do this. The army therapist just asked me a bunch of questions."

He nodded. "They tend to stick to the basics so they can check off that they did their due diligence when they only did the bare minimum. You're a soldier. You know how to answer a question sufficiently, but if that's what you really needed you wouldn't be in my office. So what brought you here today?"

I had a decision to make. Did I tell this guy the truth and rip the words out from where I'd buried them deep, or did I clam up, waste the hour, and tell Hurley I'd tried? I didn't like the idea of failure, but more than that, I couldn't stop replaying that last night with Jenna and then the look in her eyes when she ended it.

She was hurt. By me.

I'd made a lot of poor decisions in my life, but hurting her was the worst. So when it came to therapy, there was really no decision to make.

"I couldn't talk to my…girlfriend about my tour overseas, or anything else significant for that matter."

"And why do you think you couldn't open up to her?"

I scrubbed my hands over my face and then looked at him. "I don't know. She wouldn't understand what it was like. I don't want her to worry about me or think I'm crazy. I don't want to look at her and wonder if she's thinking that I'm about to snap or something. She doesn't need to carry my burdens."

He nodded like he understood. "You mentioned your time overseas first. Is that the thing that keeps you from telling her anything else?"

"Yeah."

He arched a brow. "Care to elaborate?"

I clenched my jaw. "Um…" A cold sweat beaded on the back of my neck. My pulse skyrocketed, and my chest felt tight like someone was sitting on it.

His discerning gaze felt like it was burrowing inside my soul searching for the truth, and it took everything in me not to shift in my seat.

"What happened over there?"

My gut clenched. I closed my eyes, searching for strength to finally cough up the words I'd been holding on to, and Jenna's eyes were the first thing I saw. Then her face as she'd laugh. I pictured it so clearly my heart ached.

Fuck, I missed her. If ripping myself open meant I could repair things with her, it'd be worth it, right?

"Our convoy got caught in a complex ambush." After so long being trapped, the words came out surprisingly smooth. The panic was still bubbling under the surface, and it was hard to breathe, but they'd come out.

"Okay," he said, dragging the word out in a way that told me he expected me to give him more.

The words felt like broken glass moving up my throat. "It was a really bad day."

He frowned. "Why don't you tell me what happened?"

I swallowed and rubbed my hands on my jeans. When did they get so sweaty? I closed my eyes again, thinking maybe that would make it easier to tell him, but instead, I immediately pictured that day. I had flashbacks every so often—nightmares too, but those had been less frequent since I started sleeping with Jenna. Hell, they'd been practically nonexistent as long as I slept with her in my arms until that one night that changed everything for us.

"We'd been at a local village meeting with the elders to see what we could do to help since we were planning to set up a presence there. We knew they'd be open to it because of a trusted source. Talks went well. Really well. We stayed later than we originally planned, and I was kicking a ball around with some of the village kids when our section commander told us we needed to wrap things up and get back to the forward operating base. At that point, I was the only one goofing off." I remembered that clearly. Laughing with the kids. I'd replayed that afternoon in my head so many times, wondering if things would've turned out differently if I hadn't been playing with them—if we'd pulled out of there earlier.

"We left and took the main road back to base. Things were going exactly to plan until the truck behind me exploded."

I leaned forward and put my head in my hands, the memories rushing back feeling like they were suffocating me now that I'd opened the box I'd buried them in. I'd been through a thousand trainings, but never realized how it would kick in when everything became utter chaos. We hadn't known that hit was coming, but once the truck exploded, the whole convoy stopped. The guys in my truck all looked at each other because we knew—we thought we knew—that more was coming.

We had no idea the hell the insurgents were about to rain down on us.

"I was in the third vehicle in our four-vehicle convoy when the one behind us exploded. Me and two guys from the lead vehicle dismounted to provide security and treat wounded until medevac showed up. When I got to the truck, I saw that Hurley was pretty torn up."

The words poured out of me like they never had before. "He was gripping his right thigh, but the rest of his leg was a mangled mess. I pulled him out of the vehicle and then Maxwell was there screaming about how Hinton got hit. He was another guy in the first vehicle with Maxwell," I clarified. "He was shot."

The truth was it felt like it was raining lead. The shots were relentless, all coming from the hills on our right flank. I think the only reason I was able to get Hurley out and not get shot myself was because he was on the left side of the vehicle. If he'd been on the other side, I doubt either of us would've made it out of there alive.

"Maxwell and I were in a ditch with Hurley. The vehicle I was in had moved back to offer us some covering fire while Maxwell tied a tourniquet to try to stanch the bleeding. Hurley passed out and that's when a rocket-propelled grenade hit the number two vehicle in the convoy. Two guys gone, just like that. I left Hurley with Maxwell to try to put some fire down range, toward the hillside, then ducked for cover as they shot another RPG our way. It landed a few yards away, but my fucking ears were ringing. No one tells you how *loud* everything is. I mean, you see it in movies, but those don't do it justice. It's fucking loud. So loud I wouldn't have heard a word Maxwell said to me if it wasn't for our headsets we were still wearing. His voice pierced through all the noise, and I just remember him shouting at me."

He was desperate. When the lead vehicle got hit with an RPG, we both looked at each other like this was it and he shouted. Some days I could still hear his words so clearly it was like he was screaming them in a library.

I can't go out like this, man. I never told her. I never told her I loved her.

He moved back to his hometown in Montana after he got out, and I've often wondered if he ever told her—whoever she was—but I've been too chickenshit to return his calls.

"Our last functional vehicle was hit by another RPG, and that was the moment I really thought I was going to die there. And then we heard it—fucking salvation. Two Apaches and a Chinook came over the ridge. We'd called for our quick reaction force as soon as the first vehicle blew, but it felt like we were out there for hours before they finally showed up. The Apache gunships made quick work of the fighters on the hillside while the guys inside the

Chinook gathered up our KIA. It wasn't until we got back to the FOB that I learned it had only been thirty minutes. That was the longest thirty minutes of my life. In half an hour, they killed twelve of our guys and injured one. Maxwell and I were the only ones who just had minor scrapes for the most part."

"And PTSD," he interjected softly. It was the first time he'd spoken since I started telling the story, and it made me look up to find his face filled with an understanding only a fellow soldier could have.

"Yeah," I choked out. "Yeah, and PTSD."

I scrubbed my face, pretending that I didn't notice the moisture there. I glanced out the window, desperately needing something to ground me back in the here and now.

Fuck, I wished Jenna was here. She thought she was a mess, but she was so fucking strong. I could use her strength right about then.

"You understand none of that was your fault, right?"

"If I hadn't been playing with the kids..."

His voice was gentle, but firm. "You don't know that, Connor, and it's not fair for you to carry all that loss on your shoulders. You did the best you could in a bad situation. None of what happened when you guys left is your fault. It's called survivor's guilt."

I clenched my jaw as emotion got the better of me. I brushed away another tear, not able to deny what it was this time because immediately following it was another one. My cheeks flushed with shame and embarrassment.

"Let it out, Connor. You survived. That's nothing to feel guilty over. Instead, you need to take this gift you were given and not waste it."

His words opened the floodgates and I lost it, curling forward and sobbing into my hands. That was the worst day of my life. I left that village happy and laughing and then arrived back on base in a Chinook helicopter covered in Hurley's blood, dirt, and surrounded by the bodies of the guys I'd been joking with only minutes before.

I blinked and my whole world changed into a nightmare. I hadn't viewed surviving as a gift like I should have. It was a punishment—living with those memories and nightmares. But as my emotions settled and I pulled myself back together, I was able to see things with a different view.

I was able to feel gratitude instead of guilt for surviving.

And maybe—if she'd give me a chance—I'd have a woman next to me who made this second chance worth living for.

Rule #19

DON'T SPARE YOUR EX A SINGLE THOUGHT

JENNA

There was something soothing about being surrounded by animals. The ache in my heart from ending things with Connor was still ever-present, but it didn't feel quite as sharp when I was scratching behind a dog's ears or cuddling a cat in my arms.

There were perks to working for a veterinarian.

Connor had paved the way for my internship with Dr. Cunningham. He was in his early fifties and loved his job. He always had a vibrant smile on his face, and his eyes carried a shine that reminded me of how I pictured Santa Claus. I'd been nervous for our first meeting a week ago, but once I sat down in his office and he told me a cheesy dad joke about veterinarians, any nerves I had quickly disappeared.

Now all that was left was the bittersweet ache of missing Connor. I knew I'd done the right thing for me—I couldn't be with someone who wouldn't be vulnerable with me—but that didn't make it easier to accept. Connor may not have been able to give me his words, but his actions said a lot. He'd shown me more care and kindness than any other guy I'd ever dated or been interested in.

Distance had allowed me to accept my feelings for him and acknowledge what they were. I loved him. I loved his heart, the way he took care of me and supported me. I didn't need to know his whole life story to love those things about him.

But love wasn't always enough.

And in our case, I knew I needed to know more about him, not just the things he showed me with his actions, but his past, his history. His unwillingness to tell me anything only proved that we didn't want the same things.

I put Rufus back in his kennel—he was a sweet and cuddly pug who was recovering from a close encounter with a car. He had a broken leg, but that did nothing to discourage him from trying to jump, and I found he didn't whine as much if he was being cuddled. Maybe I was too soft, but I loved being able to show unconditional affection to these precious animals who didn't hesitate to give it right back to me, even if it only happened during the little breaks I could get in between helping Dr. Cunningham.

"I'll be back to check on you after my lunch break, okay, little guy?"

He tilted his head and stared at me before letting out a small yap, hobbling in a circle, and then lying down on the soft blanket we'd placed in there.

I walked over to the set of cubbies where I stowed my belongings during the day, grabbed my purse, and then texted Sadie to confirm our lunch plans.

Since Dr. Cunningham's office wasn't far from Sadie's work, we'd managed to get lunch three times this week. It was another perk to this internship, and getting more time with my best friend like the old days had also gone a long way to soothing my heartache.

"Hey," I called out when I saw her sitting out on the patio of a sandwich place we'd fallen in love with.

"Hey, I already ordered for us."

I shook my head. I'd have to pay her back by buying next time, if she let me. She knew my internship wasn't paying me much. It was enough to cover some extras in my life while the money my dad had set aside for me went to covering my rent.

It was a hot, sunny California day, but there was a cool breeze that took away some of the repressive heat.

"How's work?" I asked when I sat down.

She took a sip of her iced tea and shrugged. "It's okay. Shannon is struggling. She's trying to hide it and she's doing a pretty good job, but there are moments I've caught her staring out the window looking a little lost. I can't even imagine how hard this all is for her."

Sadie's boss, Shannon Perry, was an incredibly accomplished woman. She owned one of the premier boutique environmental-friendly architecture and interior design firms in Los Angeles, and at only thirty-eight years old. But apparently her husband had just announced he wanted a divorce and she'd been left reeling. Since the firm was so small—only about ten employees—the news had spread pretty quickly. Sadie had filled me in on all the drama and how bad she felt for Shannon.

"She doesn't deserve this," Sadie said. "So I'm just trying to step up and take some things off her plate. Grant is too," she added right as the waiter dropped off the sandwiches she'd ordered for us. We thanked him before he walked away and then she nibbled her lip.

"I yelled at him," she said, her voice low like she was confessing.

I nibbled a fry. "Yelled at who?"

"Grant. I told him his friend was an asshole."

I dropped the rest of the fry to my plate. "Sadie!"

"What?" But she no longer looked guilty. She pushed her shoulders back like she was proud of herself. "Nobody breaks my best friend's heart and gets to live in ignorant bliss about it."

"I appreciate that, but it's unnecessary."

Her eyes narrowed. "You're not mad at him anymore?"

"I don't think I was ever really *mad* at him. I was hurt he wouldn't let me in, but I think I confused things and made our relationship more than it was."

"Don't do that," she said. "Don't diminish what you guys had. I saw you together, remember? It's okay to be hurt, Jenna, but don't make it less than it was. You loved him."

I still did.

I was worried a part of me always would.

She had picked up half of her sandwich, but she put it back down on her plate and leaned forward, her elbows resting on the table. "Would you ever give him another chance?"

"It's been over a week and I haven't heard a word from him. I doubt he wants to get back together. Why do you ask?"

"Grant's been weird since I yelled at him a few days ago. Asking questions about you without trying to be obvious about it. Like checking in on you. A part of me wondered if he was asking for Connor."

"Do guys do that?"

She shrugged. "Fuck if I know. Guys are dumb, especially guys our age. It's why I went older."

"Hey Sadie?"

"Hmm," she hummed, her mouth full of food.

"Thank you."

She swallowed her mouthful, and her brows scrunched in confusion. "For what?"

"For being my best friend. For always having my back. And maybe most importantly for just being here for me."

"There's nowhere else I'd be. Besties before testes, babe."

We didn't bring up her history of hiding her relationship with my dad—and very much putting testes before besties—but we didn't need to. I'd forgiven her for that a long time ago. I was grateful we'd found our new normal and that I still had her in my life. I couldn't imagine going through this breakup without her being there ready to help me wallow through my heartache.

Best friends were worth their weight in gold, and I would forever be grateful Sadie was mine.

Rule #20

NEVER SHOW UP UNINVITED

CONNOR

Her door was a familiar and welcome sight, but it didn't stop the swirling of unease in my gut as I approached it.

My therapist made coming here sound simple and easy, and of course I didn't fight him on the suggestion because she was the whole reason I went to therapy to begin with. But now that I was standing in front of her door after two weeks without seeing her, my stomach was in knots and my anxiety was sky high.

What if this wasn't enough? What if telling her everything didn't fix things? What if I still ended up leaving here without her?

The knots in my stomach twisted sharply at the idea. I didn't want to live without her, so I needed to find a way to convince her to give us a real shot.

I knocked on the door and shoved my hands in my pockets as I waited for her to answer—all my usual swagger completely gone.

She opened the door, her hair in a messy bun on the top

of her head with some flyaway strands by her eyes. Her beautiful hazel gaze stared at me with a guardedness she'd never had before, while mine traced every line of her face, memorizing each detail.

Fuck, I'd missed her.

"Hi," I said.

"Hi. What are you doing here?"

"I was hoping we could talk."

Hurt flashed in her eyes. "I've done enough talking, Connor. I said everything I needed to say."

She went to close the door, but I pushed my hand out to stop it. "Please, Jenna," I pleaded with her. "*I* want to talk. I just need you to listen. If..." I swallowed, not really wanting to add this part, but knowing I needed to give her an out or she'd never let me in. "If you hear me out and still want nothing to do with me, then I'll leave."

I'd leave my heart on her floor, too, but I guessed she didn't need to know that part.

She stared at me and nibbled her lip, then opened the door wider and stepped to the side. "Okay," she murmured.

I took the opening and walked in, heading straight for her couch. She sat in the small chair opposite to it, and I tried not to let it sting that she wouldn't even sit on the same piece of furniture as me.

Silence descended and she stared at me for a minute before arching her brow. Right, I guess there was no point in waiting.

"I started seeing a therapist."

Her mouth dropped open but she didn't speak, so I kept going. "After you ended things, I saw a buddy of mine from the army, and we had a talk about what happened over there. He made me realize that if I wanted to be with you, I needed to learn how to move past my mental block. That it wasn't healthy to keep it all bottled inside."

God, I felt like I was making a mess of this. That sounded like some excuse someone makes. I needed to be real with her. I scrubbed my face and then dropped my elbows to my knees, leaning forward and trying to organize my thoughts. Everything was a jumble in my head. Two weeks of intensive therapy sessions had gotten me here, but I still had to find a way to work through my body's desire to lock down and push the words out so I could win her back.

Then her hand reached out and she touched my knee. Warmth infused my entire body at that one small touch, and when I met her gaze, all I saw was kindness, empathy, and acceptance.

"Jenna—" I choked out her name and she must've seen the desperation in my eyes because she got up from the chair and crawled into my lap. I held her tight, needing her so much more than I'd ever let myself need another person.

"What happened, Connor?" she whispered as one of her hands started sliding over my short hair, her blunt nails scratching my scalp in a way that sent tingles down my spine.

"A mission went south. It was supposed to be a pretty routine day, but it ended up being a bloodbath." I talked with Dr. Hoffman about how much to tell her. I refused to put all the details of that day in her head, but I could give her the gist. There were some things you didn't need to share with people who'd never experienced war—save their innocence.

"I left base that morning with fourteen other guys and came home with only two."

"Connor," she said, her voice filled with an apology that she didn't owe.

"It took us by surprise, and when we got back to base, they gave us all a few days to breathe and then called us back to determine our next placement. I chose to come home. We were required to talk to a therapist before we could process our discharge paperwork—probably for liability reasons. But I didn't really talk. I said enough to get the approval I needed to get the fuck out of there. Then I kept my head down until my commitment was up, and I was honorably discharged a few months after the ambush. I got on a plane, landed in LA, checked into a hotel because I wasn't ready to see Grant yet, and went to a bar down the street where I saw *you*. You were the first good thing I'd experienced in a long time. I didn't want to talk about what happened because I didn't want to ruin what we had going with my shit. But it was also more than that. I couldn't talk about it with anyone. Grant tried, too, and every time I shut down."

"But that doesn't explain why you wouldn't tell me *anything* about your life. Nothing substantial anyway."

I looked into her eyes, needing her to see I was baring my soul here. "I was in the military for ten years. All anyone ever asks me about is my time in the army. No one has cared about anything else for even longer than that. My parents aren't exactly the caring and concerned types, and Grant and I have known each other so long, I never really had to explain myself. The guys in my squad knew who I was and were content with that. They didn't need to know my history or my life before we all got together. Honestly, Jenna, you're the first person who's cared enough to want to know."

"That still doesn't really answer my question," she whispered, her eyes holding all the fear I felt in my gut. She was scared of this failing too. She was scared of getting hurt. But she was the one with all the cards here.

"Jenna, I didn't know *how*. I know that seems like a weak-ass response and some bullshit, but it's the truth. I don't open up to people. I considered telling you what happened overseas, and that was the first time I'd wanted to talk about it with anyone. I think, maybe...I think I was scared of telling you too much, so I didn't tell you anything."

She got a cute little pucker between her eyes that I wanted to rub away with my thumb, but instead, I kept my arms wrapped around her, holding her close to my body. "So, you're saying you continually avoided talking about yourself at all because you were afraid of saying *too much*? No offense, but that sounds like a bunch of bullshit."

I couldn't stop the smile from lifting my lips. "Funny you say that, because I thought the same thing when my therapist suggested it. But I'm kinda thinking he was right. I *want* to open up to you. But you have this insane ability of making me feel comfortable, and I don't think there's any way I could've only shared bits and pieces without spilling my guts out to you."

"And that would've been a bad thing?" Her voice was hoarse like she was trying not to cry, and my heart ached. Fuck, I was messing this up.

"At the time, it felt like the worst thing. And my body literally went on lockdown. Whenever I'd get close to talking, I froze. I didn't know what else would happen if I had to relive those moments. I didn't know if you'd look at me differently— like I was broken or something—or if I'd even be able to look at myself. I mean, what kind of fuckhead am I to drop my shit on your doorstep when you've got enough on your plate?"

She squeezed my thigh. "That's not how relationships

work. We're in it together. I help you carry your shit and you help me carry mine. Only you were taking on mine *and* yours and not giving anything back to me. I don't want to be in a one-sided relationship, Connor. I want to know all the things about you, good and bad. And I want you to know all my things too."

I stared at her, wondering what I'd ever done to deserve her—if she'd give me a second chance. "Jenna..." I said as my voice broke. I didn't think this woman had any clue the power she held in her hands. I might seem tough and scary, but one word from her and I'd be broken beyond repair. But I still needed to ask the question anyway. She'd either give my life new meaning or she'd gut me completely. Either way, the choice was hers to make. I'd respect whatever she wanted, even if it killed me. "Is it too late to fix this—us?"

Rule #21

MAKEUP SEX IS OVERRATED

JENNA

I stared at the man I'd fallen so hard for and couldn't deny the utter fear and longing in his eyes. No man had ever looked at me like Connor did. Like I held his entire world in my small hands.

Truth was I felt like half a person without him. I hadn't even felt this awful after Peter and I broke up, and we were together for four years. But one month with Connor and my heart was all in like it'd known from the beginning that he was the one for me.

"No, it's not too late," I whispered.

He exhaled a shaky breath and then his hand was in my hair and his lips were on mine in a bruising kiss that made me melt against him. A moan escaped from my mouth as his tongue slid across my lips seeking entrance. I parted them, letting him in—more than he knew.

God this man could kiss, and I was totally sunk for him.

My fingers curled around his neck, sliding across his short hair as he pulled me tighter against him, kissing me like this kiss could fix everything. Could make us whole again.

And maybe it could because for the first time in a week, my heart didn't hurt and my gut wasn't in knots. Instead, I felt like I'd found home. Connor made me feel like anything was possible. Maybe I was letting him off the hook too easily, but he'd finally let me in, and I was willing to give him another chance. He was worth the risk.

He pulled back, just enough to drop his forehead to mine, both of us breathing heavy. "I love you, Jenna," he said, his voice strong and sure.

All the emotions that had come and gone over the last week faded to just one—love, so much love, I thought I was going to burst. "I love you too," I whispered, my voice hoarse with emotion.

He leaned forward, kissing me at the same time as he stood, carrying me in his arms as if I weighed nothing. Without breaking our kiss, he walked toward the bedroom, only stopping once he was at the foot of my bed. He laid me down gently and stood up, his body towering over mine and his heated gaze so intense there was no way I could look away even if I'd wanted to. He reached behind him and gripped the neck of his shirt, swiftly pulling it over his head and dropping it carelessly to the floor. My chest heaved as I tried to get enough oxygen because I'd always thought that move was insanely sexy. I don't know why, but Jesus, it had my panties soaked.

"Take 'em off," he said, his voice deeper and more ragged than I'd ever heard it.

"Hmm?" I asked, not sure what on earth he was talking about since my focus was on his belt buckle where his hands were slowly undoing it until one end hung loose. He gripped the other end and pulled it out of each belt loop slowly, the only sound in the room the scrape of leather over denim.

"Sugar." His rumbly voice pulled my gaze back to his face, and I belatedly realized my mouth was hanging open.

"Huh?"

"Take off your clothes."

Right. Clothes. The things separating me from feeling his hot body all over me. With moves that were nowhere near as graceful or sexy as his, I ripped off my shirt, then my bra, then shimmied out of my yoga pants and underwear until I was naked on the bed and laid out for him like a very willing sacrifice.

The right side of his mouth tilted up in the cocky smirk that got me the first night we were together, and my heart pounded in my chest.

I was going to marry this man.

Maybe it was crazy to think that after we'd just broken up and gotten back together—if you could call it a breakup when you ended your sex arrangement—but the way he looked at me like I was the only person in the world who mattered to him made me sure that it was true. He was never going to let me go, and more importantly, I didn't want him to. I wanted him to always fight for me. To show up at my doorstep and bare his soul.

His hand reached forward until he grazed his knuckles against my ankle, slowly moving his hand up my inner leg until he was leaning over me. His gaze never left mine as he switched sides and did the same thing to my other leg. My breathing was erratic, and I was sure he could hear my heart beating because the sound was so loud in my ears.

His fingers left my legs, bypassing where I ached for him most, and then skimmed up my belly. He touched me like I was the most precious treasure he'd ever encountered.

His dark brown eyes swirled with desire, hunger, and so much love, I wanted to wrap myself up in it.

"Connor..."

"I know what you need," he said, his deep voice doing twisty things to my insides. I did that to him. I made him sound needy and ragged. I made him weak as much as I made him strong. All the ways he made me feel, I made him feel.

It was a revelation. *This* was how love was supposed to be.

I couldn't keep my distance from him anymore. Wrapping my hand around his neck, I pulled his mouth down to mine, and our lips brushed at the same time that his hand cupped my breast and his thumb and finger pulled on my nipple. My back arched on the bed as a moan escaped between us.

My teeth bit his lower lip, mimicking the way he pinched and tugged on my nipple. He let out a low growl that I felt between my legs.

"Fuck," he cursed and then his mouth was on mine in a ravenous kiss like nothing else we'd ever shared.

He was done going slow. Thank God. We could go slow later, but right now I just needed to feel him inside me. I reached between us, gripping his hard length and tugging on him, bringing him closer to me. His hands were everywhere. My breasts. My neck. My hair. My hips. Touching me with such heat, I thought my body might burst into flames.

"Connor, now," I begged between kisses.

He moved away only long enough to put on a condom and then I pulled him toward me before moving my hand to wrap around his hip.

With one swift thrust, he buried himself to the hilt. "Oh God."

"No God here, darlin'. You can say my name."

I laughed. "You are so fucking arrogant sometimes."

He smirked. "You love it."

I couldn't deny it. "I do," I said seriously, and then wrapped my hand behind his neck and pulled his mouth down to mine. I knew there was more we needed to talk about, more he needed to tell me, but I wasn't going anywhere and neither was he.

He thrust into me, his hips hitting my pelvis each time he buried himself inside me as deep as he could go. "Fuck, Jenna. You feel so damn good. Squeeze that tight little pussy around my cock. Show me how much you missed me."

My pussy fluttered around him and he groaned. His dirty talk always got me close.

"Tell me who this pussy belongs to," he growled against my ear as his hand slid between our bodies until he was brushing the most tantalizing circles on my clit. "Tell me, Jenna."

"You," I cried as my orgasm crested through me until it felt like I was exploding into a million pieces.

"You're goddamn right. This pussy belongs to me. And who does this cock belong to?"

I could barely make sense of his words from the pleasure haze that was fogging my mind. He slid his hand behind my head, curling his fingers in my hair and holding my head still, forcing me to make eye contact with him as the last of my tremors faded. "Who does this cock belong to?" he whispered with a desperation that had matched mine earlier.

"Me," I said, no doubt in my voice. He dropped his forehead to mine, his chest heaving with ragged breaths as he nodded. He was so close.

"It's yours. All of me is yours."

He thrust in once more and came inside me, letting out a loud groan then continuing to rub my clit in just the right way until another orgasm took me by surprise and ripped through me.

His body dropped down beside me, and he twisted us so he could stay inside of me while his arms wrapped around my upper body, holding me close.

"I love you, Jenna," he murmured against my head. "I'll do whatever it takes to make you happy. I promise."

"I know you will. We'll both do what we need to in order to make each other happy."

"You just gotta be you, Sugar. Just be you, and I'll be the luckiest damn man alive."

I buried my smile against his chest and held him tight. I wasn't naive. I knew we'd have hard days in the future, but I also believed his promise.

We were stronger together—at least I felt stronger with him—and I had no intention of letting him go again.

Rule #22

A ONE-NIGHT STAND WILL NEVER BECOME THE LOVE OF YOUR LIFE

JENNA

TWO YEARS LATER

There was only so much teasing a person could take.

"Connor," I begged, my wrists pulling at the restraints.

God, I was so close. I needed him to let me come. He'd been edging me for over an hour, getting me right to the verge of glorious pleasure before pulling away until it had receded enough and then doing it all over again. I felt like I was going out of my goddamn mind.

My arms pulled uselessly at the straps attached underneath the bed. He'd bought this restraint system when we moved in together. My arms and legs were spread wide with very little give, making me completely helpless to him. But I loved it. In the two years Connor and I had been together, I'd learned a lot about the things I liked—and didn't—in bed. Connor was always up for exploring and pushing my limits.

It was exhilarating. And while this wasn't the first time he'd teased me with a long edging session, I was on the verge of breaking down into tears if he didn't let me come soon.

School had been exceptionally stressful this last term, and I needed him to help me release it.

"Please," I pleaded with him, but he didn't acknowledge it, just kept teasing my clit with too-gentle flutters of his tongue, getting me closer but not close enough to topple over the edge.

A tear slid free from my eyes.

"That's it, darlin'. Let all that stress out. I got you."

The tears came harder and faster—the stress pushing through the surface. I'd buried it down for the last two months while I went into survival mode to get through my classes with passing grades. I probably would've starved if Connor hadn't always had dinner ready when I came home. He'd requested a transfer to an assignment up here, which was fortunately an easy request to grant. But he somehow always managed to be home before me with dinner on the table.

He would've made an excellent housewife.

"Let it out," he murmured against my clit, his tongue lapping at me like a cat laps at cream. More tears streamed from my eyes, taking away the stress with them, but my body still felt strung so tight.

"That's it, Sugar. Fuck, you're such a good girl. Do you have any idea how fucking sexy you are?"

"Connor, please," I dragged the word out and felt his breath shudder against me.

Before I could make sense of what was happening, he was sitting up and shoving his hard cock inside me. I sucked in a sharp breath right before my entire body split apart in the most intense orgasm I'd ever experienced. I screamed as my body trembled. I probably would've thrashed on the bed if it weren't for the restraints holding me immobile.

"Fuck," he cursed before he thrust faster, rutting into

me like a man possessed. Then he groaned and came, his hot release filling my still convulsing pussy.

He sagged against me, his breathing as heavy as mine before pushing up on his elbows to take some of his weight off my completely spent body. He wiped my tears away and then kissed my cheeks, my eyelids, my forehead, my nose, and finally my lips.

"Feel better?" he whispered.

I opened my eyes to find his dark brown gaze staring down at me with love and concern. I took stock of my body, my emotions, my mental state. A small smile lifted my face —it probably would've been bigger if I wasn't so exhausted.

"So much better," I murmured before leaning up as much as I could and kissing him. "How do you always know exactly what I need?"

He smirked—that same sexy smirk I fell in love with two years ago. "Because I know you."

"Yeah, but I didn't even know I needed *that*."

He shrugged. "Clearly you don't pay enough attention to yourself."

He glanced over to the clock on his nightstand and then pushed himself off my body, slowly pulling out of me. After cleaning himself up in the bathroom, he came out with a wet washcloth, putting the warm material against my sensitive flesh. I'd fallen so hard for this man, but it was these tender moments when he took such sweet care of me that reminded me I fell in love with his actions before I ever fell for his words. When I was thoroughly cleaned, he went around the bed, releasing the straps one at a time. He gently massaged each limb as he released it, and I sagged in our bed, completely blissed out. The way he always knew how to care for me and what I needed made me feel more cherished than I'd ever felt in my entire life.

Once he was done, he slid his hands underneath me, lifting me up and eliciting a squeal. "What are you doing?"

"We're taking a shower. We have dinner reservations."

"We do?" I asked as I wrapped my arms around his neck and let him carry me into our shower. He washed my hair, something he'd told me he loved doing, and then took my loofah and proceeded to wash my entire body—thoroughly. I returned the favor, but when I tried to grab his quickly hardening dick, he gripped my wrist.

"As much as I'd love for you to do what you're thinking, we really do have a reservation."

I tried to hide my disappointment, but he caught it, lifting my chin and dropping a tender kiss to my lips. "Keep thinking what you're thinking for after dinner, alright?"

A small smile graced my face. "Alright."

We finished our shower quickly after that and got dressed. He knew there was a fancy restaurant where I'd always hoped to celebrate when I finished my degree, so I already suspected where we were going and dressed accordingly. When I finished with my makeup and came out of the bathroom to find him dressed in a suit, I knew I'd chosen the right outfit. Then again, you could never go wrong with a sexy figure-hugging red dress.

The drive to the restaurant was quick, and Connor filled the time by telling me about the latest conversation he'd had with his dad. Our parents hadn't been too happy when they found out we'd gotten together, but Connor and I both thought it was more because they were upset that we were clearly in love when they never had been. They both pretended to be happy for us now, but things had been strained. I couldn't say I was upset that my mom called me less often. If anything, it took some stress off my shoulders.

It also helped that even when she did call, Connor was

always there to hold my hand and offer me a hug when she inevitably tried to make me feel like shit for something.

His conversations with his dad hadn't been much better, but he always told me about them. Connor still struggled sometimes, but most of the time, if I asked him a question, he answered it honestly without hesitation. The only thing he still struggled with was talking about his time in the army, but since he was doing telehealth appointments with his therapist, I was less concerned about that. I didn't need to know about that trauma if he didn't want me to. He'd explained why it was hard for him to tell me, and while I didn't agree with him carrying that burden all by himself, I'd also never experienced anything close to what he had. I'd never been in a war zone, and if it made him feel better not to put those images in my mind, then I could be okay with that.

As long as he didn't shut me out entirely, we were good. And for the last two years, he hadn't.

"When will you find out how you did on your finals?"

I twist my hands in my lap. "I should find out in the next day or two. All but one class has already posted."

He glanced over. "And?"

I smiled. "Bs in every single one so far."

My internship with Dr. Cunningham had been the start of a much-needed mentorship with someone who was not only kind, but encouraging. He was always happy to answer an email or talk to me over the phone if I had questions or needed guidance over the last two years. He'd offered me a job this summer, and Connor and I were planning to move back to LA once he could get reassigned.

"What's the last one that you're still waiting on?"

"Dr. Washington's class." I was dreading that grade. She'd been none too pleased when I returned to school and requested a new advisor, but I didn't regret my decision. I needed someone who supported me, not someone who didn't believe I could do better. My new advisor was a much better fit and had even shared some additional resources for support. She shared that I wasn't the first to struggle, but several others had become very successful veterinarians and she had no doubt I would be among them. I understood some people did well with the tough love approach, but I wasn't one of them.

"You're going to pass. I know you will. You studied harder for that class than any other."

"I hope so," I mumbled to the window. I wished I had his confidence.

He gripped my thigh, squeezing it once and then leaving his hand there as a comforting touch. "I have complete faith in you, Jenna."

I wrapped my hand over his, staring at his profile as we neared the restaurant. "Thank you for all your support this year."

He glanced over, a smile on his face. "It was easy, Sugar."

My heart swelled in my chest. I still loved when he called me that.

He pulled up to the valet and then gripped my thigh where his hand still rested. "Wait for me."

I nodded and then watched him hand his keys to the valet and come around the car, adjusting his suit jacket before he opened my door and held out his hand for me.

I smiled up at him. "Such service."

He smiled back. "Only the best for my woman."

He held my hand as we walked into the restaurant. The hostess perked up when he gave his name and then grabbed two menus and gestured for us to follow her. We passed the rest of the diners, and I craned my neck behind us, wondering why we weren't eating in the main dining area.

"Uh, Connor."

He squeezed my hand and looked down on me, a knowing smile on his face. "Do you trust me?"

"Yes." There was no hesitation in my voice. I did trust him.

The hostess opened a door into a small room set up with a private candlelit table. Rose petals littered the floor, and string lights were threaded across the ceiling in a crosshatch pattern.

My mouth parted as I tried to calm my racing heart. This was so much more than I was expecting.

The hostess set our menus on the table. "The waiter will be in to take your drink orders in a moment."

"Thank you," he said as she exited, leaving us alone.

"Holy shit," I whispered. "This is so romantic."

Connor barked out a laugh and then dropped a kiss to my forehead. "Eloquently said, darlin'."

He pulled out my seat for me and then seated himself next to me. He placed his hand palm up on the table and I set mine in his. I couldn't stop looking around at all the small details.

"I didn't even know they had a room like this. It's gorgeous."

"My client told me about it."

"I love it," I said, finally focusing back on the man who made this night possible. All the stress I'd carried was completely gone, and I smiled at him hoping he could see how much I meant those words.

Apart from the waiter coming in and out only to bring us our next course, we were left undisturbed. We talked and laughed and discussed plans for the future. The food was just as amazing as I'd heard, and when the dessert was brought to us, I questioned my choice of dress. At this rate, Connor was going to need to roll me out of here.

Connor pushed the Toblerone cheesecake toward me, and I looked up at him like he had to be joking. "I'm not sure I can eat another bite."

"I've heard this is the best dessert on their menu. I'm pretty sure you're not going to want to skip it."

God, I couldn't say no to that. I loved cheesecake. I dug my fork in and took a bite, sagging back in my chair and closing my eyes in bliss as a moan escaped. "Ohmagahd," I mumbled.

Connor smiled. "Good?"

"So good," I said, already digging in for a second bite and accepting that I was going to be stuffed beyond belief after this meal. But oh my God, it was so worth it.

"What if I made it better?" Connor asked, his voice soft and almost a little shaky. But that didn't make sense. I'd only ever seen Connor shaken that day he showed up at my apartment in LA and told me about what happened to him overseas—or the condensed version, at least.

"Connor?"

He pushed the chair back, pulled his hand out of his pocket, and opened the small box at the same time he dropped to one knee. I was so grateful I'd already finished my bite of cheesecake as my fork clattered to the table and I spun to face him. "Oh my God."

He looked more serious than I'd ever seen him. "Jenna, I never knew love like this was possible, but I love you more with every day that passes. Two years ago, I wasn't sure what the hell I was going to do with my life. I was lost and broken, and like a beacon of light shining in the darkness, you arrived and lit up my entire world. You are the reason I survived that day because I was always meant to be yours. You are without a doubt the best thing that's ever happened to me, and I want to spend the rest of my life with you. Will you marry me?"

"Yes," I whispered so low, I wasn't sure he heard it. "Yes," I said louder. "Yes!" I said, nodding my head as tears blurred my vision and I threw my arms around his shoulders.

He held me tight, his laughter filling my ears before he pulled back and grabbed my left hand, sliding the most perfect ring on my finger. It was a halo of diamonds that surrounded an emerald.

"I know it's not exactly traditional, but the color reminded me of the shade of green in your hazel eyes." I looked up at him and couldn't wrap my head around how on earth I'd gotten so lucky. How did this man exist and how was he mine?

"I love you," I said, my voice watery but my smile glued to my face.

"I love you too, Sugar. Now and always."

His words seeped into my heart, and I believed them with everything inside me. We weren't going to be like our parents. This was the kind of big love that lasted a lifetime, through thick and thin.

He was mine and I was his.

Not just for tonight, but for now and always.

Bonus Rule

WEDDING NIGHT SEX CAN'T BE SWEET AND DIRTY

CONNOR

I readjusted my suit sleeves as a few more people made their way to their seats. The sun was high in the sky shining down on us, but there was a cool breeze coming off the ocean that kept us from being too hot.

We couldn't have asked for better weather for a May wedding. We were having a cliffside wedding at a beautiful resort on the coast. The view at my back was an endless ocean, and in front of me was pristine green grass surrounded by perfectly manicured bushes and colorful flowers. I stood in front of an arch that was twisted with more flowers—I couldn't tell you their names, but Jenna thought they were beautiful, so I'd made sure we were surrounded by them.

"You ready for this?" Grant asked from beside me.

"I've been ready. I would've married Jenna as soon as she agreed to give me another chance, but I knew she wanted to finish school first."

"Plus you had to prove to her you'd actually changed," he said, a knowing grin on his face.

I grinned back. "That too. But she was worth the wait."

"The best ones always are."

He would know.

The music changed, and we both turned our focus to the end of the aisle. Sadie stood there, a small bouquet in her hand as she walked elegantly toward us. My heart started racing faster in my chest with anticipation.

And then Jenna was there and I forgot to breathe.

I'd never seen a more beautiful sight than my Jenna wearing the most stunning white dress I'd ever seen and walking toward me with her dad escorting her.

I'd grown close to her dad over the past few years, and I was beyond grateful for the woman he'd raised.

The woman who captured all of my focus. Everything around me faded as her dazzling smile hit me right in the chest.

Grant's hand came to my back and he whispered, "Breathe, man."

I sucked in a sharp breath, but I still couldn't tear my gaze away. She reached me and I finally looked away from her long enough to reach out and shake her dad's hand, making eye contact so he could see the sincerity in my eyes.

"Thank you," I said, emotion already making my voice hoarse. He nodded, winked at his wife on the other side of Jenna, and then took a seat.

I took Jenna's hand in mine, giving her all my focus again. "Sugar, you look so damn beautiful."

I loved the way her cheeks flushed a beautiful rosy pink.

Who was I kidding? I loved every single thing about this woman.

"You look pretty handsome yourself." Her gaze turned

heated as it traced me from head to toe. I knew Jenna loved me in a suit—it was the one real perk of my job because more often than not, she'd jump me as soon as I got home. Sometimes I teased her that she had a thing for James Bond types. She always joked back that it was more Kevin Costner from *The Bodyguard*.

"You two ready to get married?" the minister asked with a smile.

"Beyond ready," Jenna said with a wide grin that made every thought in my head evaporate.

I didn't know what I did to deserve this woman, but I was never going to take her for granted. She was my gift for living—for surviving—and one I planned to cherish every day for the rest of my life.

Jenna giggled as we exited the elevator toward our luxury hotel room I'd booked for the night. It was a corner room known for its giant jacuzzi tub that was surrounded on two sides by windows which allowed us to see the incredible view of the ocean. As we approached the door, I stopped her and swept her into my arms—one behind her back and the other under her knees. Her arms wrapped around my neck, and her gaze softened as she stared at me with so much love.

Nothing could stop me from dropping my mouth to hers and kissing her. I'd give this woman anything and everything she wanted.

I pulled back and grabbed the keycard from my pocket. "Welcome home for the night, Mrs. Jackson."

The door swung open, and Jenna inhaled sharply as she took in the room. "Oh my God, Connor. This is beautiful."

"Only the best for my wife." I hoped by now she realized I'd always make sure she was cared for and treated like the queen she was.

She sure as hell ruled my world.

I placed her down on her feet, and she turned away from the view, pressing the front of her body against mine as her hands cupped my neck and her gaze fixed on mine. "I hope you know the only thing I need is you."

I kissed her. I'd barely been able to stop kissing or touching her all night. She was mine in every possible way a woman could be, just like I was hers.

My hands glided to the back of her dress as our kiss deepened, and I found the zipper and pulled it down until her dress loosened and fell to her feet. And then it was my turn to suck in a sharp breath as I stared at my wife in her white lingerie.

"Had I known this is what you were wearing under that dress, I would've insisted we leave the reception a lot sooner."

She smiled. "We couldn't leave sooner. We were the guests of honor."

I pulled her body back against mine. "We could do whatever we want *because* we were the guests of honor."

She shook her head, but that vibrant smile never left her face. I brushed my thumb across the apple of her cheek, memorizing every inch of her face. I wanted to memorize every second of today.

It was the second best day of my life. The first had been the day I met Jenna in that bar.

"I love you, Wife."

Her eyes softened. "I love you, Husband." She gripped the lapels of my suit jacket. "Now, let's get you out of this suit so I can drool over my sexy new husband and his hot, naked body."

A small laugh escaped as she helped me strip out of my clothes until I was left in only my black boxer briefs.

Her gaze traced a hungry line down my abs and then her hands were on me, touching me everywhere, until she was at the edge of my boxers where I couldn't hide the thick, stiff bulge. I gripped her wrists.

"Not yet, Wife. I want a taste first, and you've already got me too close to the edge. I can't let you touch me just yet."

Before she could protest, I lifted her into my arms and carried her over to the bed, placing her down gently before tugging her to the edge and dropping to my knees. I pulled her white lace panties down her smooth legs and brought them up to my nose, inhaling the scent I knew I'd never get enough of.

"Spread those pretty thighs for me, darlin'," I demanded, my voice deep and ragged. Her chest rose and fell quickly as she spread her legs and showed me heaven. She was already glistening with arousal, and I couldn't wait any longer to get her taste on my tongue. I gave a languid lick through her soaked pussy lips up to her clit and watched as her head dropped back and she let out a soft moan.

I dove in, feasting on my wife's perfect pussy, eating her out like she was my last goddamn meal, until I was sure her cries of pleasure could be heard down the hall. Her fingers gripped my hair as I slid two fingers inside her and curled up while sucking on her plump clit. Her thighs tightened against my head as her body shook from the force of her orgasm. I worked her through it until the final quakes had subsided and she sagged on the bed, breathless and spent.

I was only getting started.

I kissed my way up her body until I got to her mouth, and she opened for me, letting my tongue plunge inside and lick against hers. She let out a soft hum, tasting herself on my tongue. My girl was dirty and I loved it. She loved tasting herself on my tongue.

"I need you," she murmured.

"Give me one more and then you'll get me."

"Con—"

I cut her off by shoving three fingers into her slick pussy, and I loved the way her body immediately rose to attention. I was on a mission. I wanted her to soak the bed. I'd placed down a special blanket I'd purchased—one specifically designed for water activities during sex—when I checked us into the room before I had to get ready for our ceremony. I wanted everything to be prepped in advance because I knew I wouldn't have the patience to take the time once I got her alone.

I'd been right.

And now I was incredibly grateful for my ability to plan ahead.

I didn't take my time, but went for the gold, plunging my fingers in and out until I was hitting that spot I knew would set her off. She let out a shout and then her body was convulsing on the bed as she squirted, soaking us in her juices. Her body was still shaking slightly as I ripped off my briefs and slid home.

She sighed as I buried myself to the hilt inside her. God, she was heaven. Pure fucking heaven. I could stay buried inside her forever if she'd let me. Nowhere else felt more perfect than being connected to my wife with nothing between us, where you couldn't tell where she ended and I began.

We were one.

"God, I love you so much, Jenna," I murmured against her lips, thrusting into her, my pace steady at first, but the closer we both got, the more I rutted into her with complete abandon. She felt so fucking good—too good.

Her fingernails scratched along my back and my balls drew tight. "Fuck."

She lifted her head, nibbling my ear before saying in that sexy, sultry voice she got during sex, "Come inside me, Connor. Fill me up."

I shoved my hand between us, rubbing over her clit. I wasn't going to come alone, and I was dangerously close.

Her eyes flared and then she tipped over the edge, taking me with her. We came together, and it was by far the best sex I'd ever had.

Every time with her was the best I'd ever had, but there was something about knowing she was my wife now that made it even better. Wedding night sex was on a whole other level.

I dropped to the mattress beside her, still holding her close as we caught our breath.

"I've got plans for that jacuzzi later," I mumbled, and my heart soared at the light giggle that escaped from her.

She snuggled into me, and a peacefulness settled deep inside my bones. "We've got forever."

Yes, we did.

AFTERWORD

Despite this being the second book in the series, I actually had the idea for this book before I started writing *Only a Kiss*. I didn't know the characters, but I knew that moment of complete and utter shock when Jenna shows up to brunch only to discover the man who brought her the best orgasms of her life was her brand new stepbrother. That scene started it all. I hope you enjoyed the ride.

I couldn't create my stories without the help of some amazing individuals.

First, I want to thank my beta readers, Alyse and Kelly. Your feedback was critical in making this story shine the way I always knew it could.

To my editors, Happily Editing Anns for once again helping me clean up my story so it could be as spotless as possible (and helping me with my repetitive words).

To Kenna, Daphne, Kelly, and Ellie for being my cheerleaders when imposter syndrome hits me hard. I'm so beyond thankful for you ladies.

To my husband for your constant love and support, for

pushing me to chase my dreams, and always yelling at me to drink more water.

To my miracle babies. For always pushing me to strive to be my best for you. I love you so much.

And last, but certainly not least, to all my readers, those who just found me and those who've been with me from the beginning. I am beyond thankful for your support. Thank you for making a lifelong dream come true.

ABOUT THE AUTHOR

Cadence Keys is a bestselling steamy romance author. When she's not coming up with plots for her books, she's chasing her rambunctious toddlers around or cuddling with her husband. She loves writing heartfelt stories with relatable characters and a guaranteed happily ever after.

Learn more about her and her books on her website: www.cadencekeysauthor.com

facebook.com/cadencekeysauthor

x.com/cadencewrites

instagram.com/cadencekeysauthor

tiktok.com/@cadencekeysauthor

bookbub.com/profile/cadence-keys

goodreads.com/cadencekeysauthor

www.ingramcontent.com/pod-product-compliance
Lightning Source LLC
Chambersburg PA
CBHW030858200726
48289CB00003B/802